ENTHRALL
SECRETS

USA TODAY BESTSELLING AUTHOR
VANESSA FEWINGS

Enthrall Secrets
Copyright © 2016 Vanessa Fewings

This story is a work of fiction. References to real people, events, establishments, organizations, or locales are intended only to provide a sense of authenticity and are used fictitiously. All other characters, and all incidents and dialogue are drawn from the author's imagination and are not to be construed as real.

ISBN: 979-8-9937240-6-5
Credit: Deposit Photo Stillfx and istock photo Mehtap Orgun
Cover created by Hang Le
Edited by Debbie Kuhn

Book formatted by Champagne Book Design

I know you're tired, but come. This is the way.
Rumi

DEDICATION

For those feeling lost, displaced, or isolated, this story is for you.

ENTHRALL
SECRETS

CHAPTER 1

Chrysalis
A Year Ago

A FORCE OF NATURE KNELT BEFORE ME.

This was the best way, the only way, to describe this gorgeous thirty-something man kneeling obediently at my feet in the pose of a submissive.

Before entering the dungeon, he'd run his fingers through his perfectly combed short black hair as though reconsidering his appointment.

With some gentle coaxing, he'd removed his tailored pinstripe suit, taking his time in the luxury changing room as though trying to hold onto these last remnants of his control, working his gold cufflinks loose before easing them out and placing them carefully in a locker.

His gaze rose occasionally to meet mine as he stripped out of formality.

As a consummate professional I'd show not even a flicker of desire, no hint I was aroused by the way he'd tugged off his shirt and then removed his black pants, revealing a sun-kissed physique, a ripped torso. Perhaps he could be considered a little underweight from some unspoken trauma, but all six-foot-two of him moved with the elegance of a man who ran every day; I could see that from those lean legs and toned arms.

Just under an hour ago he'd quietly followed me into the dungeon, naked except for those boxer briefs which he'd refused to remove, providing a first glimpse of his fierce confidence, though there was no sign of conceit.

Yet.

And Jesus…

When Ethan Jones spoke with that Georgia drawl I had to remind myself I was the mistress here. The deep tone of his voice, that seductive cadence that hinted of a privileged upbringing—class, that's what he exuded. I could tell he was a man not easily swayed.

During those first few minutes when I'd worked on honing our rapport, he'd told me that his drink was bourbon "with plenty of ice"—and he'd offered me an endearing grin. I'd let him know that my drink was a nice Cabernet, sinfully chilled with a cube of ice, a scandal to any wine aficionado that I'd dilute their delicately crafted masterpiece.

That made him smile and it softened the hard lines of his face.

He'd placed his life on hold and given himself over to me for one full hour. We'd only met each other today, and it seemed out of character for this particular alpha to relent to anyone.

Yet he was here.

Reminding me of *him*…a little.

I gave my head a shake to bring myself back to the present. There was no room for melancholy.

Before the session I'd changed into my short Italian leather black dress from Barney's and pulled on my custom-made spiked thigh-high leather boots. My sleek raven hair was styled elegantly to frame my face. I wanted him to notice my sharp cheekbones and pale blue eyes, notice more than just the vixen holding the whip. I needed him to fall for me a little.

I needed to connect.

His rich cologne was being absorbed into my very blood cells, a centrifuge drawing me in with a visceral effect that put my senses into overdrive, throwing me off.

To focus, I wrapped my fingers around the chain above him as though he were still connected to it, my palm cold from tightly gripping these metal links to still them. This fantasy of us gloriously fucking would remain just that—a wild, fantastic daydream that would not be allowed to suspend the play.

He was my client, after all, and deserved an elite mistress, the very kind he'd sought out. I'd be a strict, sharp-tongued dominatrix providing moment-to-moment evidence of my world-renowned status.

He didn't need to see the real Scarlet, the sassy woman who loved burying her face in a good book—something by Deepak Chopra, Maya Angelou, or Toni Morrison—or even the poetry of Sylvia Plath. He didn't need to know I loved picnics on the beach, or people-watching in coffee shops, or that when the newbie subs arrived at Enthrall or Chrysalis, I was always the one who took them under my wing because deep down I cared too much.

No, he didn't need to know anything about me.

He just wanted to feel.

Or forget.

This innate sensitivity I'd honed over the years was essential for reaching my clients on more than just an emotional level. He needed a psychologist who dared to delve deeper and provide a visceral experience that counted.

His kind blue eyes processed every detail with intensity, and those faint laughter lines gave away his thirty years. He had this endearing way of swallowing his pride with each order I wielded as he obeyed, his head remaining bowed in reverence...most of the time.

This desire I felt to step toward him and rest my cheek against his firm chest was not exactly what he needed. He needed a dominatrix—the kind who'd not be thrown by all that southern charm.

His sudden dark, intense glare caught me off guard.

His defiance was raw and vital like the piercing note on a tuning fork. He was all tension and rippling sun-kissed muscles, glancing up occasionally to gauge my response to his continued rebellion. Disobedience I could handle.

I'd not counted on his beauty affecting me so dangerously, weakening my resolve to be just a mistress to him. The kind of connection we were experiencing was not what I'd expected when perusing his file. Whoever had profiled him had been way off. He wasn't just a suit in need of a good spanking. He was more...so much more.

Those dark curls were now a tussle of damp luscious strands. A series of whips and paddles had left his flesh tinged a deep shade of red as he'd writhed in ecstasy against the Saint Andrew's Cross, his moans reaching beyond the four walls.

I saw pride reflected in his eyes, and I raised my chin high.

"Stand."

He rose with that familiar majesty, almost arrogance, even though I noticed he was not necessarily a man of excessive means—seeing that Michael Kors watch he'd peeled from his wrist earlier. However, from the way he'd recognized that Onesti ram sculpture we'd passed on the way in I could tell he was educated. To me that was more impressive than any financial status.

I was surrounded by men of privilege and yet I was far more interested in the wealth of the mind, the kind of conversations that enlightened and brought meaning to life.

The scent of his expensive cologne mingled with the aroma of fresh leather cuffs and I breathed him in, letting those sensations overwhelm me.

He was waiting patiently for his next command, standing with his hands behind his back, his head bowed.

It had only taken a few seconds to ascertain which room would be best. The décor was sleek and simple so his mind wouldn't wander too much, a dark dungeon drenched in a soft red hue. Still, coaxing him to open up was proving to be a challenge. He'd been soothed initially when first restrained, as subs often are when handing over their control.

Though from the way he pulled back from surrendering completely, trancing-out would be an issue for him.

I gestured with my whip. "Back to the post."

He folded his arms.

I took a short step toward him. "Problem?"

He was fighting me again, showing me a devilish grin.

God, he really was a pretty boy and that scar on his jaw added to a bad boy image he couldn't quite pull off.

I suppressed a smile. Switching wasn't an option. That fantasy would have to wait for when I was alone. Later, I'd be vibrating my clit to the max with all thoughts trained on him—anything to get him out of my mind.

And out of my system.

It took all my will to resist crushing my lips against his, flicking my tongue inside and tasting his mouth fully, which would be a fair revenge. A good mouth-fucking for the way his flirty eyes undressed me every chance he got.

That subtle shift in his demeanor hinted he'd perhaps caught on to my momentary fantasizing. His brow arched in intrigue.

So far my sub had endured his punishment well, with toned muscles flexing in time with the rhythm of the horse whip. No way could he be described as a seasoned bottom. He didn't even close his eyes during the process. His jaw clenched as he endured it. He emitted an occasional growl of resistance…a long moan now and again.

I re-secured him to the steel cross, facing forward with his torso against the metal post and his beautiful ass in my face.

How easy it would have been to press my body against his, my tight leather dress one with his pink, firm flesh. With a tug I checked to make sure his wrists could slip out easily if he desired. He'd requested easy-free restraint in his contract. Getting out of these would be possible—though a punishment lay on the other side of disobedience. And he knew it.

When I used the paddle on his buttocks he leaned forward with his arms pulled back, a trickle of perspiration running down his spine and over the rippling muscles of his taut back.

"Should have gone in first." He shook his head as though rising from a dream.

"What was that?" I circled around and stared into his midnight blue irises.

"What?"

"You mentioned something about going in first?"

The four inch heels on my leather boots ensured I matched his height, our lips dangerously close. He leaned toward me and I stepped back to avoid his kiss. His jaw flexed in frustration.

"You have to earn the right," I chastised.

"Jesus, Scarlet." His dazed expression morphed into iciness.

There was an irregularity in his mood and something in his tone that hinted of rebellion. I was no stranger to defiance. But this was different.

He was different.

He stood straight and shook off the moment as though I'd had no effect on him. With every move I made he maneuvered masterfully to resist subspace.

His reaction to my voice didn't reflect a man who'd been a member of this scene for years, as he'd told our admissions officer at Enthrall. He'd looked surprised when I'd dragged that bullwhip across his torso—and his gaze had locked onto mine, as if in warning that he might use it on me.

I pointed at the floor. "Crawl on all fours around the room."

With a smirk, he slipped out of the restraints and stepped away from the cross. He sank to the floor and began to crawl forward in an erotic display of subservience.

The softest sigh escaped my lips as I enjoyed the scene of having such a primal creature relent to my orders.

The art of dominance in any form is to accept the power handed over by the sub and then lead them into the center of bliss and hold them there indefinitely. This man refused to totally surrender. Or even erotically enjoy the scene. This was clear from his lack of erection. And at no time had his pupils dilated. Not one sign of arousal.

Yet he'd openly admired me, drinking in my curves, his gaze lingering on my ample breasts. And that lick of his lips proved he wanted to take me.

He gave his head a shake and it seemed that frustration seeped from his pores as though annoyed that he couldn't get there; for him there was no rising to the occasion.

I was self-aware enough to know I'd catch any man's eye. My daily runs along Manhattan Beach, which were a stone's throw from my condo, kept me fit and Pilates kept me lean. Nutrition and a truck load of sunblock held back the years.

Way back when I'd studied psychology at Harvard I'd paid for my tuition by modeling underwear, no shame there. At first I'd refused all that money left to me in a lover's will, though later I'd come to accept his gift, realizing the good I could do with it.

I'd gotten into the kind of adventures worthy of a wild child during my college years, including an adventure in Paris amongst France's most erotic masters.

I couldn't think of that now.

Couldn't let the memories of those unbridled months of happiness derail what was meant to be a finely tuned hour.

I'd been taught by the very best.

And even now I worked under Dr. Cameron Cole, a brilliant psychiatrist and the man who'd navigated me through those delicate years. He was the director of Chrysalis, and a man I counted as one of my dearest friends. Ironically, he'd have this client cracked open like a nut in seconds. My approach was always gentler. Cameron's idea of nuking a mind was always a last resort.

The art of a session was our ability to comprehend the root of the problem, and whereas all other forms of therapy had failed, our results were legendary. We healed, changed lives, and returned love to the loveless.

I was considered an internationally sought after mistress, having clients fly across continents for the pleasure. So this client's continued rebellion felt skewed, considering he'd personally requested me. Frustration lingered deep in my gut because he hadn't submitted to me yet. A failure foreign to me.

He pushed himself to his feet.

"Did I say you could stand?"

"God, you're beautiful, Scarlet."

"Mistress Scarlet," I snapped. "Back to the cross, now!"

He moved over to it with a careless swagger—the only sign of arousal was that fiery look in his eyes.

I got closer. "Tell me how I can help you."

"Perhaps if you use your mouth?" He arched a brow.

"I don't do that."

He shrugged. "I tip well."

"One more outburst and I'll demand silence from you."

He narrowed his gaze. "Everything else you've done has fallen short. I'm close to asking for my money back."

What the fuck?

"Mr. Jones, we discussed my role at the beginning."

"Can I spank you?"

"You requested a domme."

"Yes, but my fantasy is to spank a dominatrix." He dragged his teeth along his bottom lip, and lowered his eyelids seductively.

No way was I breaking the rules.

I knew better.

That kind of intimacy occurred between a sub and master at

Chrysalis only when the director signed off on it. Relationships got complicated and everything at the club was finely orchestrated and based on science. It's what made our society unique. A well-balanced structure that was led by a brilliant psychiatrist who saw to it that all play ran smoothly. Safety remained a priority.

He looked devastated by my silence. "You don't find me attractive?"

"Of course. Now on your knees."

His glare intensified.

"Don't make me repeat it." A wave of doubt came over me…a sense that not everything was as it seemed. "Tell me your thoughts. What's holding you back?"

"Nothing."

"Clearly it is." I gestured at the door. "Session's over, Mr. Jones."

His jaw tensed and he seemed to be working through a thought. "Someone I loved very much was shot dead in front of me. Since that day…" He lowered his gaze.

My heart flinched with pain at this haunting memory he'd been brave enough to share. This was the trauma affecting his sexuality.

"When?" I asked.

"Four years ago."

"What happened?"

He swallowed. "Can you help me?"

"I believe so."

"Let me touch you."

I shook my head and stepped back.

"Why?"

"We don't do that here."

"But you're touching me?" He leaned back and reached out to either side of the Saint Andrew's Cross and slid his wrists back into the leather cuffs. "I need to be touched, Scarlet."

I knew what it was like to lose a loved one, to feel powerless as they were ripped from me, the unfairness of life overriding my dreams and sabotaging my happiness.

What he was asking was such a little thing. Easy, really.

If Cameron had taught me anything it was that there was a gray area that occasionally warranted exploring. Sliding my hand down past his waistband, I cupped his balls first, and then gripped his length, beginning that gentle gliding motion to get him hard.

And get him into subspace; the place where those occluded emotions would begin to clear and then heal.

"You can stop now." The starkness of his voice forced my hand away.

He slid his hands out of the cuffs and sidestepped me. "My name's not Jones. I'm a District Attorney and I'm going to make sure there's a warrant issued for your arrest, Scarlet Winters."

I stared at him in disbelief. "What? We didn't do anything!"

"I'm actually trying to be your friend here. Might wanna listen."

"I don't understand."

"Money was exchanged."

I sucked in a deep breath. "No, you're a client."

"Who runs this place? I want their name."

I shook my head, thoughts swirling in confusion. I felt a dreadful sense of betrayal at the threat of having this cruel man in the center of our sacred space.

"You know what happens now," he said.

Defiantly, I placed my fisted hands on my hips.

"LAPD are on their way. They'll rip this place apart. And if you think your life is bad now, Scarlet, wait until I've finished with you. Make it easier on yourself and comply."

"Who are you?"

"Get your phone. Make the call."

"I'm escorting you out."

"Scar—can I call you that?"

"No." *You can fuck right off.*

"Great hooker name by the way." He stepped forward. "I want to know who's in charge of this place."

"You can't bully me."

"Give me what I'm asking." His gaze lowered to my lips. "Or suffer the consequences."

A cruel reminder of the manipulation I'd confused for chemistry. His jaw clenched as he leaned in to kiss me. He was so close—that intoxicating cologne sparking my arousal and lowering my defenses all over again as his lips brushed mine. He took my mouth fiercely, his tongue plunging inside as though his threat hadn't been spoken. I responded to his kiss, fighting with every part of my will to draw back the power.

Ethan pulled away and shook his head. "That didn't happen."

"I can help you."

He measured his words. "I have everything I need."

"For what?"

"It must end, Scarlet. This place. It's over."

"Who are you?"

"Ethan Neilson." He headed off toward the door. "Now if you'll excuse me, I have to wash off your fucking perfume."

CHAPTER 2

CAMERON'S EXPRESSION HADN'T WAVERED AND THAT familiar "calm in a storm" attitude I always drew strength from remained a constant as he strolled toward me through the foyer.

I'd paced beneath the low-hanging crystal chandelier, trying to stifle my panic and wondering who was going to make it here first: the LAPD or the Director.

Luckily for us it was Cole.

Within half an hour of my phone call, Cameron had walked through the front door of Chrysalis with the command he was known for, without any cruel accusations of blame—just a hug for reassurance.

Those who underestimated this thirty-three year old stunner of a man were fools. Cole's black short, mussed hair and perfectly chiseled features enhanced his ability to enforce supreme domination. The tailored suit that rounded out his tall, well-defined frame, along with his highly professional demeanor, proved he was a powerhouse of control.

I'd helped Cameron evolve Chrysalis into our sacred sanctuary, and it was not lost on me that I could be responsible for its downfall.

He led me into an alcove for privacy. "Where is he?"

"Your office."

He ran a hand through his hair. "Not alone, right?"

"Dominic's with him."

"The staff?"

"All left. Except for Pilar." I glanced back at the front door. "What are we going to do? The police are going to arrive any second."

Cameron held my shoulders. "I'm here now."

I leaned against his chest again and closed my eyes as he wrapped his arms around me. Ethan's threat had rendered me too distraught to think straight.

That asshole was about to meet his match.

Cameron Cole ruled this empire with an ironclad fist right alongside his best friend, Richard Booth, both of whom were not only masterful dominants in their own right but also brilliant men. Cameron was also the Director of a Beverly Hills psychiatric practice—and if that wasn't impressive enough, his father was a world-renowned tea baron. Cole's fortune made Richard's wealth look tame. Richard was the Assistant Director and ran Enthrall, our smaller club in Pacific Palisades. He'd say he dabbled in stockbroking but in truth he'd turned all of the employees' savings into impressive profits. He gave his time and expertise freely.

Whereas Richard's father had gone down in history as a villain of Wall Street, Richard had proven you really can make a shitload of money by being honest.

Though I'd soon be losing my condo when I had to pay for the legal team I was going to need.

Walking through hell was inevitable.

"How did Neilson book a session with you?" Cameron's voice was calmer than I deserved.

"He was screened at Enthrall."

"Who by?"

"Sandra Reynolds. H.R."

"We can stop the hemorrhage at least."

"You'll fire her?"

"Afraid so."

"Ethan's going to close us down."

"Well, we've had a good run."

Nausea rose in my throat and I turned on my heel and made my way down the hallway.

Bursting into the restroom, I leaned over and retched into the sink, anger rising that this stranger had turned our world upside down with his insidious attack on all I held dear.

Goddamn it, people needed this place.

Strong fingers trailed through my hair and pulled it back from my face. "It's okay, sweetheart," soothed Cameron. "I've got this."

"He's going to send me to prison." I struggled through a wave of panic.

Cameron stared at my mirrored reflection. "When have you ever known me to fail you?"

Those were more than words. That was Cameron's call-to-arms. And not surprisingly he wouldn't waver, wouldn't show any weakness. I'd never known him to lose a fight and if I knew one thing about Cameron Cole he never lost hope.

"Wash your face. We have work to do."

I splashed my face with cold water, and when I braved a glance at my reflection again I hated the distraught look still in my gaze. I'd always prided myself on bouncing back quickly from the crap life threw at me, but this was out of my league.

Cameron handed me a soft linen napkin.

Taking in all the gold-plated faucets, trimmings and marble tile, I felt another wave of guilt. This place had cost a fortune to furnish. Chrysalis was a place of luxury and wowed anyone privileged enough to make it over the threshold. Black and burgundy drapes and low-hanging chandeliers rounded out the decadence. This was one of the world's most opulent clubs and we hosted political leaders, sportsmen, CEOs, A-list actors, and even royalty. Our members were ensured privacy and very often undertook the kind of sessions that healed their childhood traumas and returned them to society as highly functioning individuals.

No one was ever supposed to know of their connection to us. That had been our promise from the start and Cameron's ingenious management ensured it.

"What are we going to do?" I asked.

"Tell me about your time with him."

I threw the soiled napkin in the basket. "It was our first session. It was going okay right up until he dropped the bombshell of his true identity."

"Any irregularities before that?"

I swiped a stray hair out of my eyes. "He wouldn't submit. No subspace."

"Interesting."

"Why didn't they send an undercover cop?"

"Doing the job himself means no one fucks up. He's a control freak. Now, was there anything else I can use?"

"He mentioned a loved one being shot in front of him. Used it to manipulate me into touching him. Lying bastard."

"Did you perform a sexual act?"

I slapped a hand over my mouth.

"Oh, come on, Scarlet, it's me you're talking to." He gave my arm a comforting squeeze.

"I broke the rules."

"Are you kidding me? I'm always breaking them."

I looked away. "I touched him."

"His dick?"

"Yes."

He mulled that over. "Did he come?"

"No. I touched it for ten seconds. He never once entered sub-space. No arousal whatsoever."

"No erection?"

"No."

"At any time?" He arched a brow.

"No."

"Gay?"

"Alpha as they come." I shook my head, trying to help with his troubleshooting, but was too nervous to see a way out.

"Tell me more about that event in his life."

"He mentioned something about wishing he'd gone in first. Didn't make any sense. He mumbled it to himself. Looked like he was working through some private issue."

"Neilson used the truth mixed with a lie to convince you to break the law, which is entrapment." Cameron pulled out his phone and scrolled down the screen.

"He's going to ruin me."

"Oh, shut up." He winked at me. "I've already ruined you. And you loved every second of it."

A thrill fluttered through my chest—a momentary break from torment. "You're looking to see if there's anything on him?"

"Come on, Scarlet. This will be fun. You know how much I love a challenge."

"Are you going to fire me, too?"

His eyes rose to meet mine.

"I deserve it."

"Scarlet," he snapped. "He could have been a psychopath. And you were alone with him. Am I angry? Yes. But not with you."

I leaned over his shoulder to see what he was reading on his phone's screen. "Is that him?"

"Well, look at that. L.A.'s finest."

"You couldn't have profiled him that quick?"

"I kind of feel sorry for him."

"His wife was the one shot in front of him?" I read on in horror. "The murderer got off on a technicality. How the fuck did that happen? So much for justice."

"Guilt's a cruel bastard, isn't it?"

I rested my head against his arm. "What are you going to do?"

"What I always do. Psych the shit out of this."

CHAPTER 3

C AMERON INVITED ME TO STAY IN HIS OFFICE WITH ETHAN.
He'd asked Dominic to leave and his moody attorney
had hesitated at first, but then had complied with his wishes.
No doubt he was off to put together a legal brief that would be set
in motion as soon as the police got here.

Cole offered me a reassuring smile and gestured toward the seating area at the rear of his office where a circle of ten leather chairs faced in on each other. He chose to sit and I sat beside him.

I usually loved it in here with all the high shelves stacked with medical compendiums and books on psychiatry. An antique oak desk with carved legs sat in the center, squarely on a Persian rug. Old photos of respected therapists hung here and there on the walls.

There was a complex structure in the corner that could flip a sub upside down. Scattered about were antique accoutrements that had once served as barbaric therapies. An old rope from a straightjacket, or the antique thumbscrews Richard always coveted and threatened to steal.

I shuddered, thinking how all of these rare collectibles could be lost because of Ethan's attack on us. He had no understanding of what we did and his arrogance made him a great threat.

Neilson lingered at the back of the room, fidgeting with his shirt collar. He'd probably dressed in a hurry. His hand slipped into his right jacket pocket to retrieve his cufflinks and he weaved them into the buttons neatly. When he raked his fingers through his hair it made him look more vulnerable.

He'd stepped into the lion's den and he knew it, realizing he had nothing left to lose.

Piping hot coffee was being served by Pilar, Chrysalis's loyal housekeeper. After setting the tray of three mugs and a plate of freshly baked cookies on the coffee table, she was ready to go home—well before the police got to question her.

She gave Ethan a nervous look and then left.

From the way Ethan kept checking his watch, it seemed he, too, was wondering where the police were. He strolled over to the Chinese cabinet and opened the door.

I gave Cameron a wary glance but he seemed unconcerned. He had every right to shut down Ethan's snooping until he handed over a search warrant, but he didn't seem perturbed by his inquisitiveness.

Ethan reached into the cabinet and removed the small leather saddle. "What's this?"

The erotic design of a small cock gave away its use, and as he turned it over he frowned in realization.

Cameron dropped a cube of sugar into his coffee cup and stirred it.

"People strap this to their back?" asked Ethan. "Why?"

"A form of punishment during horseplay." Cameron smiled. "As you can see, for the rider the punishment turns into pleasure. The rider can't get off the galloping stallion so they have to endure forced orgasms."

"This lifestyle of yours is not only fucked up, it's obscene." He shoved the saddle back into the closet.

Cameron took a sip. "Matter of perspective."

"What about STDs?"

"We use protection. We screen."

"Glad you're admitting what this place is." Ethan sat opposite us and leaned forward with his elbows resting on his knees, as though ready to spring up if needed.

"What do you believe this place is?"

Ethan waved his hand through the air. "Private club. Exclusive members. Debauchery." He glanced at his watch.

"They're not coming, Ethan."

"Excuse me?"

"The police."

"You think so?"

"I know so."

"If that's true," he said, scowling, "and you have members with that kind of power, go ahead and inform them I'm taking them down too."

"Cookie?" Cameron raised the plate. "They're home baked."

"Laced with drugs?"

"That would be unethical."

"Cole, you can expect to be prosecuted."

"Perhaps I can offer you a free membership?"

Ethan glared at him. "You have an issue with reality?"

"Let me speak frankly, Ethan. I'm going to run through the reasons why we are so important here."

"Feel free. Talk away."

Cameron's genius was legendary, and having seen the way he worked I'd also learned a few tricks. Still, Ethan wasn't going to be dissuaded—and if I could see that, so could Cameron.

This would be a waste of time.

"In 1965," Cameron began, "a small boy in France was locked in a cupboard by his mother. It actually ended up being for the first twelve years of his life, which I'm sure we can both agree was bad. Now, this boy was incredibly smart…"

He was talking about one of my dearest clients, Monsieur Trourville, who continued to have sessions at Enthrall. Our relationship was sacred. I squirmed in my seat, unhappy that his story was being shared with this asshole.

Cameron continued. "As you can imagine, the abuse, which included a great deal of violence, rewired his brain. After his mother's funeral he continued to live in the same house. He didn't leave it for another fifteen years. His agoraphobia was debilitating. While he was trapped in that cupboard, he was given a flashlight and some books to read, including an encyclopedia. He read it from cover to cover— memorized the damn thing. His I.Q. is well over 165."

Ethan scoffed. "So he's a client now? This place cured him?"

"We did."

"Are you a doctor?"

"Yes, I am."

"Psychologist?"

"Psychiatrist." Cole sipped his coffee. "But I digress. Our client's treatment was so successful he emigrated here and began working on groundbreaking discoveries. Many of them proving Einstein's theories. He's also a great chess partner. Do you play?"

Ethan refused to answer. He leaned back and crossed one leg over the other in relaxed arrogance.

"Well, we know you play the saxophone," said Cameron.

"Bravo, Cole. You read my bio."

"I did, and I'm sorry about your wife."

"So you read tabloid fodder?"

"The L.A. Times ran a piece on you. You like to give drug cartels a run for their money, apparently. But it backfired, so shouldn't you be in hiding? Under police protection?"

"I don't run."

"Quite the risk."

"Is that a threat?"

"Does it feel like a threat?"

"Yes."

"It's not. I'm too sophisticated to use such a banal technique. Perhaps feeling threatened comes from a self-punishing mechanism? Guilt wields a mighty sword. But you already know that."

He leaned forward. "Me being here has nothing to do with my wife."

"I disagree."

"Seriously? You believe it's appropriate to go there?"

"Subconsciously, you know I can heal you."

"I'm all good here, thanks. There's nothing wrong with me."

"Your therapist failed to cure your erectile dysfunction, Mr. Neilson. Apparently, every form of therapy you've sought out has resulted in failure. You've given up. Luckily for you your subconscious mind is still in the game. It brought you here."

He threw me an angry look.

I pressed my hand to my chest in sincerity. "Please, we can help you."

Ethan gripped the armrests. "If you're referring to me not responding to a prostitute during my time in that sordid playpen, you're mistaken."

"How dare you," I snapped.

"Scarlet." Cameron raised his hand to silence me. "This is his weak attempt to elicit an emotional response."

He was right, of course, and I needed to remember not to respond with a kneejerk reaction. Cameron could have rolled off my qualifications to Ethan and told him I was, in fact, a Harvard grad with honors, but he wanted to protect me.

"Ethan, why did you come here?" I asked. "You could have sent someone else."

"Scarlet's made a very good point," said Cameron. "Why not just send an undercover officer?"

He shot to his feet. "You can't manipulate me. Or blackmail me. What I went through with my wife is nobody's business. If you think

I want to spend one more second in this shithole then you might want to read those—" He pointed to the bookshelf. "You are way off base if you believe you can play games with me."

"Here's what I'm offering," said Cameron. "I'll waive the membership fee of a quarter million, which you'd never be able to afford on your salary as a D.A., and I'll personally take you on as a client. Let's get your dick back in action."

Ethan was stunned into silence.

And so was I. My heart raced as I tried to figure out how we were going to correct this error of judgment.

Ethan glared at Cameron, then turned on his heel and stormed toward the door.

I jumped to my feet. "Ethan, please. Wait!"

He slammed the door behind him.

My gaze fell on Cameron.

He smiled up at me. "Well, that went better than expected."

CHAPTER 4

MY ONLY OPTION WAS TO GO ROGUE.

I pulled into the parking space outside the District Attorney's office, here on Temple Street in downtown L.A., and reassured myself that I was the best person to handle this mess. Ethan and I had connected in that dark dungeon—I knew this in the depths of my soul. His passionate kiss had proved it way more than words ever could. He'd crushed his lips to mine in what had felt like a desperate yearning, and what followed had revealed an unmatched craving for both of us. I'd seen evidence of this in his eyes, even as he'd verbally challenged me.

I recognized that spark of obsession.

A hint of what could be.

This plan to come show up uninvited was either a stroke of genius on my part or I was unwittingly breaking the law. I was going to talk my way into Ethan's office and beg him to see what Chrysalis really was—not the sordid club he believed it to be, but a thing of beauty, of healing. It was a sanctuary, a place I considered my second home. Our clinic had saved so many people who would have otherwise fallen by the wayside.

Though Cameron would hate me for it, I was going to offer my sincere apology for his behavior, too. He'd gone too far this time. His brilliance needed reigning in.

I'd dressed conservatively. Hell, I'd put on jeans and a sweater and gone all cute with my hair in a ponytail to add to this girl-next-door look. I even wore my favorite Ugg boots, which held off the chill of the late afternoon.

I looked up and saw Ethan strolling across the parking lot. I shoved my keys back into the ignition and tracked him until he climbed into a Toyota Land Cruiser.

Shit, I'd missed him.

He was quite possibly heading home for the day. After that grueling sparring session with Cameron this morning he'd no doubt had his fill of stress.

I knew it was wrong to stalk him. Wrong in so many ways.

And Cameron would never need to know.

I hit the gas and my Lexus took off after Ethan's Cruiser. Keeping my distance, I followed him out of the car park and tailed him through traffic—all the way to Sherman Oaks.

We drove along Ventura and up Knobhill Drive, and I mused darkly that the name of the road was strangely appropriate for the bastard.

He pulled into a short driveway and parked. Staying in my car a little way down from what looked like his house, I ran through all the possible scenarios of how he'd react to seeing me again. The only way this would work was if he gave me a few minutes to explain. At least my way was gentler than Cameron's.

Speaking of Mr. Bossy, his ringtone blared from my iPhone.

I pressed it to my ear. "Hey, I'll be right back. I'm running a few errands."

Cameron scoffed. "What are you up to?"

"How do you know I'm up to something?"

"You don't do errands. You have your subs do them."

I'd learned long ago that lying to Cameron was a bad idea. "Look, I know I can salvage this. It was my fault Ethan got into Chrysalis. I'm putting this right."

"Are you at his office?"

"No."

He paused for a second. "I don't doubt your negotiation skills, but he's a loose cannon. You need to let me handle him."

"I graduated with honors from Harvard too, Cameron."

"One word, or should I say country."

"No you don't." I was twenty back then, for goodness sake.

"Still gonna say it. *Paris.*"

"Fuck you."

"If I did decide to copulate with you, I'd enjoy fucking you. And remember, you would have ended up in dire straits if it wasn't for me."

"We both remember how that little life-altering charade went. It changed me forever."

"You're welcome."

"Your ways are what some would consider to be fucked up."

"It's my pleasure to serve."

I scoffed. "I can do this."

"During your session with Ethan you sensed something was off, yet you continued. You're attracted to him. And while I believe you'd make a cute couple, right now that attraction is clouding your judgment."

"I see his goodness."

"So do I."

"I've come all this way."

"You're at his house?"

"At least let me try."

"What's his address?"

"Sherman Oaks."

"Where?"

"Knob Hill. Nice neighborhood. Oh, there's a puppy. Oh my God, it's so cute." I watched the dog being led away on his leash by a young woman out for a stroll. "It's a pug."

"Scarlet, it's too soon. Ethan must sleep on our offer. I need him to wake up tomorrow morning having realized subconsciously he has no other choice."

"That's what you got from the way he stormed out of your office?"

"Visiting Chrysalis was his cry for help, even if he doesn't know it yet. This information must find its way from the prefrontal lobe to his limbic system—"

"And then on to his brain stem. I'm familiar with the science."

"He's lonely, Scarlet."

"Yes, and these are the kind of clients I'm best with."

"Don't go in."

"I can make him see sense, Cam."

"I'm coming over there to get you."

I ended the call and dropped my phone in my handbag, shoving it under the seat. Then I got out of my car and locked it.

I made my way up to what I assumed was Ethan's driveway, passing his Land Cruiser parked out front. I admired the modest home set back from the street. This was actually a nice location with a quick walk down to the boulevard. Though in L.A. traffic, the commute might be quite an ordeal unless he left extra early.

The front gate was open, which led me to think he didn't have a dog. The front door was open, too. I wondered if he'd noticed me following him and this was a warning that he knew I was here. A power play, perhaps.

I stepped to the side of the door and peered through the window, cupping my hand against the glare of the late afternoon sun in order to peer into his lounge. Cozy rugs complemented the polished hardwood floors. A curved wall divider separated this room from a hall.

His furniture appeared new and had a natural look. The light wood and plush cushions were evidence of a woman's touch.

My heart ached for him even after everything.

The psychological damage of seeing his wife murdered would last a lifetime. Our Ethan was a complex man and this event had no doubt affected him in a myriad of ways.

Unfortunately for us, he'd gone on a superhero bender that had no end in sight.

I sucked in a long breath, trying to feel confident, and went on in. "Hello?" I called out.

Ethan came round the corner carrying a glass of amber liquor, ice clinking. He'd removed his jacket and tie and his white shirt was hanging casually over his pants.

His eyebrows rose in surprise.

I stepped closer. "I was hoping we could talk?"

"How did you get in?"

"The door was open."

He looked annoyed. "Yeah, right. I'm respectfully asking you to leave." He reached into his pants pocket and pulled out his Smartphone. "This is a serious mistake, Scarlet. You know better."

"Your gate was open, too."

"No, it wasn't." His thumb brushed along his screen. "I'm calling the police. I suggest you leave."

"I just wanted to say how sorry I am. We should have treated you with respect. No matter what happens, please say you'll forgive us."

"I know you like handcuffs. So this shouldn't be too much of a stretch—"

"At least let me finish speaking!"

He lowered his phone.

I gave a nod of thanks. "What happened to you was terrible. Worse than terrible. I'm so sorry, Ethan, because I know you're a good man. You stand for justice, for human rights. I know that your first impression of us was negative, but we're good people, too. Clients come to us after all hope is lost, with all sorts of conditions. Yes, we party at Chrysalis because we're also a community of individuals who care deeply for one another. Cameron really does believe he can help you."

"Finished?"

Instead of answering, I gave him a pleading look.

"Good, now get the fuck out."

His hateful glare made me avert my eyes.

"Please," I said.

"I'm not averse to physically escorting you outside." He lowered his gaze. "If I have to."

I turned to leave.

The mirror behind him shattered.

I flinched as his drink exploded in his hand, liquor splattering his shirt, shards of glass scattering across the room.

In the chaos, I followed his lead and dropped to the floor, my shoulders hunched and my hand up to protect my face from any more flying debris as I crawled behind him toward the arched wall. Ethan reached over and grabbed the back of my collar, dragging me alongside him down a hallway.

I gasped for air, fear nearly paralyzing my lungs. Some fucker was using a silencer.

Dust rained down on us as the ceiling fan came unhinged. It crashed down, knocking Ethan forward as he tried to shield me. It struck his back, shoving him headfirst into the wall and cracking his skull against the brick.

He slipped to the floor—out cold.

"Jesus." I stared down at him, at the trail of blood trickling from his brow.

I scrambled to lift his ankles and then dragged him backwards down the hallway, my breathing ragged and my heart pounding with the strain. He was slim but he still weighed a ton. His blood left a trail on the hardwood floor behind us.

I'm not fucking dying in this house.

A sob of terror caught in my throat.

I kicked open the first door I came to and dragged Ethan inside the room. Then I slammed and locked the door, and flipped on the overhead light. When I saw the desktop computer and a bookshelf chock-full of law books, I realized we were in his office. A green Hulk figurine sat atop a stack of old comics.

I fell to my knees and rolled Ethan onto his side. Then I ran over to the phone on his desk and lifted the receiver.

The line was dead.

Shit. Shit. Shit.

I'd left my phone in the car.

The bulb flickered and went out. The only light now was flooding in from the full moon.

On all fours I felt my way back to Ethan. "Wake up." I shook him hard.

Something slammed against the door so fiercely it caused the wood to crack.

"Ethan, please," I begged.

The words Cameron had spoken found me in the dark. "*I'm coming to get you.*"

CHAPTER 5

Harvard Years

"I'M COMING TO GET YOU," SNAPPED CAMERON. "WHERE THE hell are you, Scarlet?"

"I'm ready for this." I rubbed my jetlagged eyes. "You have to trust my judgment."

"You're not going to Le Maison de Plaisir. We've been over this."

"Too late." I leaned against the wall, next to the phone. "I'm already here."

"Paris?"

"Just landed at Charles de Gaulle Airport." Turning, I glanced at the line of cars to see if my Rolls Royce limousine had arrived.

The moon looked majestic in the starlit sky, and I felt as though it welcomed me. Visiting this exhilarating city was like a dream come true. And I was so proud of myself for having taken this leap of faith.

A recent downpour had left pools of water sparkling on the pavement; the scent of fresh rain lingered. Car horns blared—the hustle and bustle of travelers coming and going, their fashion so elegant, so

chic. I regretted wearing my worn jeans and short jacket. At least I'd
prepared for the chill by donning my woolen scarf.

Anticipation curled in my chest. This felt so right.

At twenty, I couldn't drink at home but halfway across the world
I'd be knocking back Cointreau and cocktails as much as I liked.

Cameron sighed heavily. "I should have known you were up to
no good when you dyed your hair auburn."

"Forgive me?"

"I'm calling Monsieur Francois. He won't let you in."

"Okay."

"Not worried?"

"I can't hear you," I blurted out. "There's a plane taking off. Hold
on."

A 747 engine roared overhead.

The thrill of hearing Master Cole's domineering tone of voice
fired me on. I'd always gotten a kick out of riling him up. Though this
was by far the most daring adventure I'd ever embarked on, and I'd had
some pretty wild weekends with the other subs from D'envoûtement,
Cameron's club in Harvard Square.

I'd proven I could play the perfect submissive, that I'd experienced
the best training and served my masters well. I'd loved every luscious
moment of being subjugated to the extreme.

Still, there was that cruel unspoken truth: only a submissive who
graduated from the most exclusive house in France was thought worthy enough to serve the society's elite dominants. If I pleased them
I'd earn my promotion. I'd come back a dominatrix.

Cameron had told me this was a myth, but I knew he was trying to protect me.

He really did have a way with words, an artful persuasion when
changing the subject. Apparently he was being wooed by the Psych
Department at Harvard to study psychiatry. They were trying to lure
him with compliments that would make any student blush, saying

he had a promising career equal to that of Sigmund Freud himself. Cameron was mulling it over, taking it all in stride.

Like most brilliant men, he hid his kinky side well—more to protect those who came to find solace in his sanctuary.

He'd also been the one who encouraged me to apply to study at Harvard, after he'd learned I was waitressing at the city's most popular bar, despite my G.P.A. of 4.0. Before meeting him, I'd been traveling around the States with no real direction. Seeing my potential, he'd pulled some strings, which had morphed into a miracle. I was about to become a psychology major, starting my freshman year at Harvard in the fall.

If I was even still alive by autumn.

I had set my sights on darker adventures—the self-destructive kind.

Like giving up and giving in to my death wish.

And right now my only saving grace was D'envoûtement.

But I wanted more...

And I'd asked for a referral to Paris's illustrious Le Maison de Plaisir. Cameron had refused me. He'd also broken my heart when he'd declined to train me himself. He didn't think I was ready for *him*.

"You're not prepared for those kinds of extremes," he'd warned, shutting down my request. "You need to work through some personal issues first. Open up. Let me in."

Didn't he know there was no doorway into my heart? Just a black hole where pain languished—the only respite my time with him.

But I'd found another way.

There was always another way.

While being here I would prove him wrong. I would, without doubt, make my mark on this community. From the highbrow clubs of New York and L.A. to here, my dream destination, I'd prove myself worthy to top with the finest.

Cameron was one of the most famous of all the doms, his reputation among the best. His talent for the dark arts made him both feared and admired. He'd taught me so much, like how to enter sub-space, how to dress as a premier sub with merely a thong and a col-lar, and he'd even taught me how to cook. One favorite lesson was how to mix up a dirty Martini, extra dry, and then watch with pride as my dom savored it. Oh, and another was learning how to give the best bareback blowjob. Though, much to my annoyance, I wasn't giv-ing it to Master Cole.

He'd refused to take me on personally, giving the excuse that I was like a baby sister to him. Despite my frustration, it was the first time in my life I didn't feel let down or used because of that. But it still didn't stop me from wanting him.

My love went so deep I'd do anything for him.

Except obey.

I'd always lived by my own rules. No matter how hard he'd tried to contain me he couldn't. My barefoot wildness would always endure.

I'd come a long way from that teenager who'd experimented with her foster parents' LSD. The drugs I'd consumed had dulled the pain of the bruises left by those the state had paid—and trusted—to watch over me.

I told myself I was no longer that girl who pined for her parents' attention, winning every school spelling bee and crying afterwards when no one came to watch. There was certainly no family to cel-ebrate with me when I'd earned a scholarship to study at Harvard.

I'd gotten hired at the Russell House Tavern, and it had only taken a month for me to get into mischief. After overhearing the whis-pers from customers who'd not realized I was listening, I'd learned about a private BDSM society, located conveniently near my studio apartment. Later that week I'd climbed in through the back window of D'envoûtement and fallen at Cameron's feet.

Literally.

The rest was history.

Another plane flew overhead and I had to press the phone closer to hear.

"Still there?" he said.

"Yes."

"Listen to me, Scarlet. We're talking about a level you don't even know exists. If you think your fantasies are dark, wait 'til you hear theirs. These men are not to be toyed with. For starters, they'll pierce your labia with a steel tag. Do you want that? Because that will be the least of what they're going to do to you."

A wave of doubt fell over me. "You told me I was the best submissive you've ever trained. I want to transform into a mistress. You told me a visit to France is the only way."

"With me. Not alone. You have your master beside you who knows your limits and can cease the play when you can no longer talk. This is a place where you don't get a say."

My sex flinched with the thought of that total power exchange.

"I'll refund your flight. You have Harvard to prepare for. I've promised your lecturers that you have the maturity to earn your place at one of the most prestigious—"

"I'd only be here for a week."

"You think you get to dictate the timeframe?"

"I signed a contract."

"Well, I'm going to have Francois shred it. He won't let you in. So walk back into the airport and I'll arrange your flight home. First class. You're in Europe so you'll get served champagne and fresh-baked cookies. Or biscuits. Or whatever the hell they call them. Now how does that sound?"

"I'm not going to Le Maison de Plaisir."

There was an awkward silence.

"Cam, are you still there?"

"What are you talking about?"

"I'm going to Madam Delour's."

"No, Scarlet, listen to me." He sounded panicked. "This is a bad idea."

"But it's all arranged."

"By whom?"

"I'm not telling you. You'll get angry."

"Let's talk this through first. Okay?"

"It's decided."

"Don't get in the Rolls."

"How did you know they're sending one?"

"Because that's how it's done."

I thought him cruel for trying so hard to stop my adventure.

He made a rude noise. "Tell me you didn't go through De Sade?"

"He's been good to me. He's been there for me."

"You spent time with him?"

"Kind of."

It had been a session like no other. De Sade had punished me so very much, but I had deserved it. That scar on my thigh was testament to how hard he'd pushed me. Cameron need never know about our session—De Sade had told me that.

During those hours with him he'd revealed our community's darkest secret: there was one other man besides Cameron who was a true master. He could unravel my secret and splay it open—rid me of this death wish. He would be able to reach inside and save me—if I willingly gave myself over to him. This man was capable of promoting me.

No, don't let Cameron ruin your chance.

I'd had no choice but to take this leap of faith. De Sade had warned that in forty-eight hours the placement would be given to another submissive if I didn't get on that plane. And there were so many subs in line. It would take years to get another invitation as prestigious as this one. Turning down this honor now would jeopardize any future chance.

Of course I'd run right home from work after telling my boss I wasn't sure when I'd be coming back. I was warned my job might not be waiting for me. But this was a gamble worth taking. My destiny was a magnet pulling me towards possibilities that were impossible to resist.

I'd quickly packed and then left an envelope on the kitchen table containing next month's rent for my roommate, so he wouldn't be short. Hours later, De Sade had turned up at my studio apartment with my first class ticket—one way until my return date had been finalized. It was always done this way, De Sade had explained to me. All I had to do was say "yes" to leaving right this second.

"No regrets," I whispered to myself.

The shiny black Rolls appeared out of the darkness.

"Scarlet, can you hear me?" Cameron asked.

The limo idled on the curb in front of me.

My heart fluttered. This was really happening. "I have to go."

"No, no, no, don't hang up—"

CHAPTER 6

France

I SLAMMED THE PHONE INTO ITS CRADLE AND SNATCHED UP MY backpack, running off toward the shiny black Rolls.

I knew it was wrong to be rude to Cameron, especially after all he'd done for me, but he wasn't going to change my mind. Giving him the chance to talk me out of this wasn't an option.

The gray-haired chauffeur had a handsome face and a smart hat. He walked to the rear passenger door of the Rolls and rested his hand on the latch.

"Hello, sir," I said, shifting the weight of my bag. "I'm Scarlet Winters."

"I know."

"How?"

"I have your photo."

His hand hadn't moved from the passenger door.

"Shall I get in?"

"I'm waiting."

Did I need a password? I hadn't been provided with any.

He tipped his hat and took my bag. "Remove your clothes."

No, he didn't just ask that of me.

I was tired and hearing things and this was all so new. I glanced back at the many travelers arriving and leaving and then turned to face the chauffeur again, trying to read his expression to see if he was serious.

Self-doubt tightened my chest as I mulled over the possibility that his request was some kind of test—a proof of loyalty like no other.

I'd flown all these miles and earned Cameron's displeasure for it. Still, when I returned to his club as a dominatrix I'd be the toast of D'envoûtement.

I stared at the limo's blacked-out windows, wondering who was waiting inside.

"Listen to me, Scarlet. We're talking about a level you don't even know exists. If you think your fantasies are dark, wait 'til you hear theirs."

Exultation rushed through me at the thought that I'd finally been given the chance to shine alongside the finest submissives. De Sade had seen my potential and promised me a referral to the highest office in Europe. Letting him down wasn't an option.

Fuck it.

I pulled off my sweater and then unzipped my jeans, sliding them down over my hips, removing them. I kicked off my pumps. The ground sent a jolt of ice into my soles. Gritting my teeth, I slipped off my lacey underwear, feeling the eyes of the driver on me the entire time. I hugged my clothes against my chest.

Standing completely naked, I willed him to open the door before I broke some dreadful law. I knew the French were open-minded but this was insanity.

I refused to glance back and face the people who might be staring at me.

The chauffeur gave me a nod of approval and opened the limo's door.

I lowered my head and scurried inside.

My breath caught in my throat when I saw the beautiful young man sitting at the far end of the leather seat. He looked to be in his late twenties. His hazel eyes held mine and I was caught off guard by his striking features. A refined nose and high cheekbones made him look like he came from aristocracy. He closed his newspaper and placed it next to him on the seat.

I was sure this was Monsieur Danton Belfort, the man De Sade had told me about. I'd been warned about his strict rules and controlling nature. His discipline was legendary.

A wave of giddiness hit me. He was here to greet me and I knew what an honor this was. The pressure I felt to please him was greater than I'd expected. Still hugging my clothes to my chest, I used them as a shield to cover my body, too shy to show off my nakedness to him just yet.

His piercing gaze felt like it entered my soul, as though somehow he knew my darkest and most daring fantasies.

De Sade had warned me. *"He is profoundly talented at punishment. He is a cruelty you will come to crave."*

Rebellion thrummed low in my belly.

Show me your cruelty, and I'll show you my power.

"Monsieur…Danton Belfort?" I asked softly.

He gave a sharp nod, glancing over at the stern-faced black woman who sat across from him. She looked to be around forty years of age, and was absolutely stunning in that French chic way— wearing leather and thigh-high boots, her red lipstick glistening on her full lips.

How I wanted to be *her.*

A pretty young blonde submissive, around my age, sat at her feet with her head resting on her leg. The girl's silver collar was attached to a long, thin chain and she was looking up at Madame with an expression of adoration. She had on a delicate thong and her nipples were so very pert.

The chill reminded me of my nakedness and I sat up straight, trying to look obedient. This was what I'd always wanted, to take a chance like this and own my sexuality.

"Are you Madame Delour?" I tried to pretend this was a normal conversation and I wasn't sitting here stark-naked.

She threw a wary glance at Danton.

I wondered if I'd ever look as threatening as her.

The pretty sub at her feet gave me a friendly smile. She lowered her eyes and settled into a luscious trance.

Every cell in my body came alive, tingling with the call of sub-space, the thrill of the dare. I felt the wetness between my legs as my gaze roamed over the handsome man whose eyes held mine. This was my new master and he was magnificent in every way. Those intelligent eyes were assessing me, his head tilted as though deep in thought.

The limo still idled at the curb.

Something was expected of me. I laid my clothes on the seat beside me and placed my hands on my lap.

After another minute of silence, I breathed out to ease the tension and slid to my knees.

I bowed my head. "Master, I am here to serve the House of Madame Delour."

"I hear you're well-trained?" His silky French accent caressed me, his tone deep and distinguished. Yet, as he held my gaze, I sensed a kind of sadness…a yearning.

"Yes, sir."

"Your invitation was actually from the House of Hillenbrand."

I nodded, trying to understand what this meant—afraid that one glint of doubt would give me away.

"De Sade sent me," I said softly. "He says I'm ready."

Danton chuckled. "Let's see." He began speaking in French and though I didn't understand him, I knew he was talking about me.

He gestured for me to come closer. Pushing myself up, I bent

over and moved past the mistress and her sub on my left, reaching
him at the other end of the car.

I crouched before him, waiting patiently to be invited to settle
at his side.

"*Enivrante*," he whispered.

I wished I knew what that meant.

He reached for his zipper and freed his cock from his pants.

My heartbeat fluttered at a million beats per second as I realized
the intimacy had begun.

Already?

"For you," he said.

I hesitated, not moving.

He leaned closer to me and wrapped his hands around my waist,
the warmth of his palms feeling welcome against my chilled skin. He
turned me around to face the front, and my thoughts ran wild hoping I had what it took to please him. With my arms outstretched to
steady me, I lowered myself onto the tip of his hard cock.

"You may," he said.

I sank down onto him and he filled me, stretching me wide until
I was completely impaled. I sucked in a loud breath.

This was too soon. We haven't even left the airport…

No. This merging wasn't soon enough, and to prove it to him my
sex squeezed him tightly, adapting to his width.

"Very good." He shifted to better position himself.

His approval made me giddy with happiness. I relaxed as he
eased my legs apart, going slack against him, leaning back and feeling
proud at how beautiful we must look to the dominatrix and her slave.

Monsieur Danton gripped my thighs. "No, Scarlet, nice and still."

My short, sharp breaths rose above the thrum of the engine, my
erotic pose a display of a new master accepting his submissive. He
explored my breasts with his delicate hands, tweaking my beaded
nipples. I forced myself to remain still as his fingers trailed down to
my sex and pulled back my folds.

My clit ached to be touched.

The other submissive was led on her chain toward me. She knelt, poised between my thighs, her stare locked on my sex, so close she could easily see me stretched wide and twitching with pleasure around my master's formidable cock.

Madame gave the chain a gentle tug forward and the submissive's head came closer, her tongue reaching out, ready to pleasure me.

Rocking my hips forward, I tried to close the gap between us.

Danton tutted his disapproval.

I stilled.

His foreign words flowed like a dark poem, soothing me. I clenched him tighter with my sex and brought my arms behind my back to pose with my wrists together.

Waiting…

"Proceed, Solene," ordered Danton.

I shuddered with pleasure as the tip of her tongue brushed along my clit, causing ripples of ecstasy so intense across my sensitive flesh that I clinched my thighs.

My master pulled them apart again.

Madame's hands came down on my sex to ease apart the folds for Solene.

"Thank you, Mistress," Solene muttered, and began lapping at my clit again.

"More tongue," her mistress commanded.

The tension in my thighs made them shake. Danton's ability to sit quietly while I squirmed and writhed was admirable. I was trying to obey and not ride him no matter how strong the urge, doing my best to prove I could pass this first test of obedience.

Solene continued lapping at my sex with exquisite passion, moaning as she suckled. My respect grew for her with each flick of her tongue as she coaxed me closer to climax.

The bliss I was feeling finally unlatched me from my control. I became a frenzied mess of need, thrusting my hips wildly towards Solene's mouth as my clit begged for more.

My moans grew louder and I slapped my hand over my mouth to suppress a scream as I came, the intensity of the blinding orgasm snatching my breath away. Danton's hands wrapped around my waist and his hips rose as I slammed down upon his cock. He allowed me to have all of him in a show of generosity.

When it was over, I was left shuddering, my sex stretched around my master's girth as Solene lapped at my wetness to bring me down.

"She's too willful," said Madame.

My heart sank with those words.

"We can tame her." Danton eased me off him.

"Yes," I whispered. "Tame me, master." I flung my arms around him and nuzzled into his neck, breathing in his musky cologne—his scent of sexy supremacy.

He truly was beautiful and so very like a dark, mysterious prince.

Together, cheek-to-cheek, we looked down between his thighs and watched Solene lavish affection upon his still erect cock.

Jealousy rushed through me at seeing another being allowed to perform this act upon my master. He had failed to release inside me. I yearned to take him in my mouth and be responsible for that delirious look on his face, instead of her.

Danton's sharp eyes held my envious gaze. "Soon, *ma chère*. First, you must meet the others."

I wondered who "they" might be. Other submissives? Girls who'd become my friend and perhaps fight me for my master's love?

Cameron had told me I was too feisty, too jealous, too wild to be the best sub a master could have, and I'd screamed at him that it wasn't so, that I'd prove him wrong. He'd merely given me an arrogant smile.

Solene was sucking my master's cock too slowly.

Another wave of envy hit me and I had a sense that controlling this, controlling Danton's pleasure, would endear me to him. Reaching down, I grabbed Solene by her lustrous blonde locks and gently forced her into a quicker rhythm. She groaned against his shiny tautness, and I felt him shudder.

Up and down I guided her, harder and faster, so that her mouth worked an elegant and yet furious pace on my master's cock.

She took him deeper into her throat and glanced up for my approval, as though I were the master of this scene.

I leaned in and crushed my lips against Danton's, kissing his mouth wantonly as his tongue responded to my forwardness. His groan of pleasure proved he was enjoying Solene's brilliant efforts under my expert guidance, her sucking louder now as she worked him furiously.

I exulted in the knowledge that we were bringing Danton dangerously close to climax. His tongue suddenly went rigid and still as mine fucked his mouth in time with the sub. This fast rhythm was stirring her most primal desires, setting them loose. Her mouth ravaged him with bliss, proving his erection had become the center of her universe, his orgasm her obsession.

Bewitched by unmatched pleasure, Danton's head fell back, his eyelids closed and his jaw slackened.

A sigh of disapproval came from our mistress, but I ignored her, not letting up as my continued strength proved my domineering edge.

His tongue fought to steal back control, overwhelming my mouth, forcing me to relent to him. I obeyed his demand and he grunted into my mouth, his body stiff against mine. I closed my eyes, mesmerized by the exotic scene of him coming hard in Solene's mouth, his body shuddering, his hips thrusting upward as she swallowed all of him.

I pulled back, loosening my grip on Solene's hair, playing with a golden strand as she finished him off with delicate licks.

Danton crashed back against the headrest and stared straight ahead as though trying to gather his wits.

I helped Solene tuck his cock back into his pants and then secure his zipper.

His beautiful fierce eyes held mine, and I felt as though I were waking from an erotic dream.

Then I pulled away, realizing what I'd done. I'd stolen the power and made it my own.

My mischievousness had three witnesses and I'd just revealed my true nature. My future with them was quite possibly over before it had begun.

"Master." I lowered my gaze and dragged my teeth over my bottom lip.

Silence lingered...

Again, my eyes rose to meet his. Silently, I begged him to let me stay.

"She's an impossible conquest," Madame said, her tone verging on anger.

Danton brushed away an auburn lock that had fallen over my eyes. "She is perfect." He lowered his gaze to meet mine. "We promise to tame you. Would you like that?"

"Yes, sir, more than anything." I crushed my lips to his.

CHAPTER 7

France

ANTON CHOSE ME. *ME*.

This realization felt like a sword slicing through the old binds of self-doubt that had imprisoned me all my life. I was worthy of him.

And I, too, had chosen this man as my master and given myself willingly.

Being here was also proof that I was in charge of my own destiny. Crawling naked on the ground, all I could think of was that I'd finally made it to the house of the elite. Danton had a reputation as being one of the finest doms, and being with him filled my soul with happiness—making it easier to ignore the gravel biting into my hands and knees as I made my way toward the large house.

Danton strolled majestically beside me.

It was no surprise I'd fallen asleep beside my new master on the way here. A blanket had covered me, and I'd felt Danton's comforting hand resting upon my body all the way. At some point I'd heard the opening and closing of the car door as Solene and her mistress had left us alone.

I yearned for my collaring ceremony and for my new master to officially make me his.

I had no idea where we were or how long I'd been asleep so I couldn't guess the time we'd spent driving through Paris. Perhaps, had I not closed my eyes, a blindfold would have been placed on me.

I'd never know.

On my hands and knees, I climbed up the cold steps of the manor. Moving on ahead until I was inside, I passed through a lavish foyer with expensive dark wood furnishings, many of which looked like antiques. The hardwood floor was easier to crawl on. A sweeping staircase lay just ahead. This was exactly how I'd imagined a *chateau* would look, with its old-world style and homey decadence.

On the left was another door and to my right a hallway. The door stood ajar, and peering through I saw a large library with leather furniture and shelves stacked full of books. The room was drenched in a yellow light that beckoned me.

Perhaps I'd be allowed in there to explore. I so hoped I would be given the run of the house and be able to make myself at home in between my chores as a sub.

This was it. I was really doing this.

No going back.

A soft sigh escaped my lips and my body trembled with anticipation.

The scent of fresh-cut flowers lingered in the air—and something else—a rich aroma of spices. A masculine scent muted by tones of amber. Cologne?

"Stand."

With my chin high and my arms behind my back with my wrists held together, I posed obediently. Master Danton stood behind me and his chest felt firm against my naked back. He reached around and with his closed fingers he brushed them fast across my nipples until they beaded and flushed, causing a wave of arousal that shocked my sex and made it throb.

My moans echoed around us.

Before Cameron had attempted to rule me, no other man had even tried. Even De Sade had merely taken me through my paces and stated I was a lost cause. Yet here Danton had taken me on, wanting to test the endurance of my sexual hunger, which knew no bounds.

He wanted to heal and free me. Cherish me.

I leaned forward as I neared climax.

The intense pleasure reached a fever-pitch. My nipples perked at the constant strumming, feeling a delicious soreness. I was groaning now, this never-ending play teased me onward, an invisible string tugging between my breasts and my pussy, making my clit throb.

"Master?" I needed permission to come.

"Silence."

A jolt of fear slithered up my spine.

They appeared from all corners—one, then two, until I counted at least ten men surrounding us. All of them were handsome in their own way, dressed in tuxedos. I could tell they were all alpha males by the way they walked, their intimidating statures conveying a startling strength.

Their fierce, intelligent eyes focused on us, and I saw that familiar reflection of lust in their gazes. High-brow warriors ready to ravage.

My cheeks burned bright red. I was on display like an instrument, yet my arousal grew unabated.

Danton whispered. "I'm presenting you. Don't come, slave."

Moaning, struggling for self-control, my head fell back against him and I writhed at these sensuous sensations surging through me, pressing my breasts into his palms and trembling with ceaseless ecstasy.

He let go and nudged me forward, knowing full well he'd revved me up perfectly. He'd left me so primed, verged on the razor sharp edge of need, my sex screaming for salvation from this dreadful yearning.

Oh, my God, am I meant to be with all of them?

Reality hit me.

Ragged breaths left my lungs as the seconds passed, as I saw their arrogant expressions and the inevitability that I was theirs for the taking.

What the hell had I signed up for?

I struck a confident pose, refusing to be owned by anyone but Danton.

Rising out of an erotic trance, I spun around and stared into Danton's eyes. His hazel gaze held mine, his irises warmed with gold flecks.

His nod confirmed my fear.

My breath caught in my throat. My fate was about to be snatched out of my control.

"Where are the others?" But I knew...

"Others?"

"The other subs?"

He tutted his answer.

No.

I fell against him, crushing my forehead to his chest with my eyelids squeezed shut. I finally understood Cameron's warning. I'd believed I could endure anything they'd do to me, any ordeal forced upon me, but this was so far from what I'd imagined.

Danton pried my knuckle-white grip off him and turned me around.

He nudged me forward toward them.

The room was silent except for my sharp gasps of apprehension.

Surrounded by these testosterone-fueled males, I swooned with uneasiness. Despite their beauty, despite them having been carefully screened, these men of class and obvious distinction were not what De Sade had promised.

Having trained at D'envoûtement, I'd witnessed senior subs taken by more than one partner but nothing like this. These men were like fierce lions and I'd stepped right into their den.

De Sade had set me up for their pleasure and Danton was not only my master but the one who had delivered me to them.

In my mind I heard Cameron's wisdom. *"When in doubt draw on your sacredness. Empower yourself from within."*

I'd observed my brilliant master, Cole, as he'd guided his sweet subs through their training, and having aspired to be his equal I'd observed every one of his actions during the sessions I'd been permitted to sit in on. I'd devoured each second witnessing his expert domination.

The art of masterdom.

"I should be with you," he'd warned me during our last phone call.

How I yearned for him now.

Think. Draw on all you've learned…all he's taught you.

"Bow before me," I commanded. "I am your new mistress."

Feeling a powerful rush of excitement, I wallowed in this moment knowing without a doubt I was ready to hold court and take command.

I hoped I could sustain this level of power just long enough to find where they'd stashed my fucking passport in case I needed it.

Their expressions were unreadable and so far they'd not moved.

My confidence grew. I said seductively, "I will bestow great pleasures on those of you who obey. Now down. On your knees. All of you."

Danton stepped before me and blocked my line of sight. His expression was difficult to decipher. But, if I had to guess, he looked pissed off.

I placed my hands on my hips.

He glared at me. "What are you doing?"

"I'm taking ownership of this house," I said. "Now bow."

Danton's angry gaze bore into mine.

I smiled proudly. "I haven't finished."

"Oh, you're quite finished." Danton grabbed my arm and led me up the sweeping staircase as a string of beautiful French words flowed from his mouth.

Something told me he was swearing.

CHAPTER 8

France

A CASCADING SHOWER BURST OVER MY BODY, WARMING ME, and I used this precious time to rethink everything. Reconsider what the fuck I'd gotten myself into.

I wasn't alone in this glass cubicle. Danton had stripped off his clothes and joined me in here, his bossiness continuing unabated.

With my hands splayed on the glass in front of me, spine arched, butt out and toward him, I endured the endless spanking he was giving me. There came an extra snap against my flesh as water sparked with each strike. Tranced-out dreamily, I was on the verge of coming. Now and again his hand missed a cheek and struck my pussy, and I rested my forehead on the glass willing him to miss again and again.

And he did. His palm met my sex so many times in exquisite whacks of pleasure that it sent me reeling.

"Sorry, Master." I turned my head back to look at him.

He reached for a sponge, squirted soap on it and proceeded to brush it over my sensitized bottom. He ordered me to turn around and told me to place my wrists together behind my lower back. He washed between my legs, teasing me. I swooned when he eased apart my labial folds and caressed me there.

He threw me a stern look when a moan escaped my lips.

I went silent again, trying to endure the way he flicked the sponge against my clit.

We were both being pummeled beneath the hot water, an intimacy I continued to yearn for. I also needed to see his forgiveness for my outburst downstairs.

My pulse raced faster when I thought about having to face those men again and what they might do to me. I'd never been fucked by more than one man before. I trembled at the thought of how the rest of my day would be.

Literally fucking painful.

Danton seemed distracted and was rarely making eye contact. It had been a challenge to not reach up and cup my palm to his beautiful face to try to get his attention. His naked sculpted physique was tall and lean, and the fine lines around his eyes aged him beyond his thirty years. There were a few small bruises on both his upper thighs and I wondered if he'd gotten them from too-rough a play. My gaze fell upon his erection bursting out of dark curls.

I yearned to taste him there.

His frown deepened. "Explain what happened downstairs."

I wiped water from my eyes.

"There was reticence, Scarlet. No, there was more than reticence. There was fear? This concerns me."

"Are they all here for me?"

"Of course. This doesn't please you?"

I tried to form the words that were frozen on my tongue. Fear grew into a lump in my throat I couldn't swallow, but I didn't want to disappoint him.

He looked away. "I know you don't like me very much—"

"I do," I burst out. "I like you an awful lot."

He didn't seem to believe me. "Either way, that's not any concern for the purpose of the house. What were you thinking? Addressing your masters so rudely?"

"It felt like the right thing to do."

"Clearly, it was not. Now, let's discuss how we will move forward. I will supervise you for two days only. When you sleep, or eat. When you walk about the house. When they fuck you. Then after that I will be replaced by another dom who'll watch over you. Turn around please."

I obeyed with a shudder and he lifted my hair off the nape of my neck and used the sponge to caress me there.

I spun round and looked up at him. "But...all of them?"

His expression changed to uncertainty. "This is what you asked for in your written request."

"What request?"

"Your contract. Your submissive's fantasy?"

"I'm not sure what you mean."

"De Sade sent it here." He gave me a ghost of a smile. "I understand that a fantasy feels different as it unravels in reality. We'll guide you through this process. We promise to honor your desires."

"Why can't I just skip all of this and get right to my promotion?"

"You asked for this. Flew all the way from America—"

"I didn't request more than one master."

His hand stilled and the sponge hovered over my belly.

"I only want you." I wrapped my hand around his full length, and he felt like iron wrapped in satin. I felt him twitch against my palm. I considered dropping to my knees and taking him in my mouth to show him how much I wanted to be his.

His cock felt like salvation.

If I could just get him to possess me as his alone.

He got even harder and my gaze rose to meet his. I licked my lips, wondering how he'd taste.

"God, you're beautiful," he whispered. "But I would never be enough." He gave a nod as though this was decided.

"But you are."

"No, with me there are complications, Scarlet. I am only here for a while. I'm not staying. I promised to see you settle in and become comfortable. I told De Sade I'd greet you at the airport. See you safely here. This was a favor to him, you understand. A courtesy."

I let go and leaned into him, resting my head against his chest.

He wrapped his arms around me. "This is what you requested. Full emersion. Many masters."

"But I'm only used to one."

He pulled back and frowned.

There was something in his stare, as though a serious thought had occurred to him.

"What's wrong?" I said.

"Will you do something for me?"

"Anything." *Just don't leave me.*

"Sign your name on the glass."

"Why?"

"Do it."

I faced the shower door and with my index finger I squiggled through the misty steam:

Scarlet Winters

Danton's eyes widened when they saw how I'd written my name. "Turn around."

I faced the glass and rested my palms on the panel, standing still. His hands roamed over my buttocks and then slid between my cheeks, spreading them a little, moving closer to that delicate rosebud that was puckered tight. I jolted when he slipped a fingertip into my ass and held it there. My muscles clenched him.

"Scarlet?" he said. "You've never been taken like this ever before?"

"No, not yet." I squeezed my eyes shut, shocked by his intimacy, feeling thrilled as his finger explored as though gauging its tautness. I flinched at the pressure.

"De Sade has lost his mind." He removed his finger and ran his hand under the water and then turned off the faucet.

He opened the glass door and got out.

I followed him.

Danton's cold demeanor remained while he dried himself off. He wrapped a towel around his waist and then refocused on me.

Raising my hands high I let him dry me off and then dress me into a short see-through nightgown. He led me back into the bedroom and again I tried to come to terms with the fact that this would be my private room for a few weeks.

The four-poster bed was rigged out with chains folded neatly above it, silk ties hanging ready from the bedposts. Before my shower, I'd explored the dark wooden cabinet in the corner and had found so many accoutrements I was already acquainted with—and a few I wasn't.

Danton continued to ignore me while he put on a smart tuxedo, buttoning his pristine white shirt. He slipped into a pair of highly polished black shoes. My master looked so handsome as he arranged his bowtie. He combed his hair, glaring at his reflection as though annoyed with something.

Me, perhaps?

I had, after all, made a scene seconds after arriving. Instead of kneeling before the men of the house I'd gone rogue.

Danton moved with such a refined grace that he was mesmerizing to watch—his masculine control giving him a regal appearance. I didn't want him to leave. I already felt bonded with him. I trusted him.

And why had he asked me to sign my name in the shower?

"Have I upset you, Master?"

He sat beside me on the edge of the bed. "The contract I was sent had a different signature."

"I didn't sign anything."

"I know that now."

"What does this mean?"

"These men are ready to devour you." He turned to face me. "This is not what you want?"

Swallowing hard, I tried to understand why De Sade had done this to me. Was this some kind of revenge? A vendetta between him and Cameron that went way back?

I looked away from Danton, too nervous to answer.

"Shit," snapped Danton.

"Have I done something wrong?"

He spewed out a string of foreign words that sounded laden with frustration. "Cameron has condemned you for my sake."

"No, Cameron didn't want me to come here. It was De Sade."

"De Sade works for Cameron."

"Then why would Cameron seem so upset?" I said. "He told me not to get in the car with you."

He closed his eyes, but not before I saw a flash of pain. "I should never have told them."

That didn't make any sense.

A shudder ran up my spine as he looked away from me.

What did he mean? Did Danton have a penchant for doing cruel things to his subs—worse than De Sade?

"Master, you are the only one who can help me have a break-through, help me transform into the finest dominatrix."

He cringed. "They are so cruel."

Was he really going to hurt me that much? My chest tightened with apprehension, yet I felt relieved that we were discussing this matter, at least.

He shook his head solemnly.

"Cameron loves me," I reasoned.

"It seems he loves me more."

"How much pain?"

"I don't want to hurt you."

"I'll try to obey. Maybe you'll use pleasure, too?"

"Don't you see, Scarlet? You are already trained."

"They told me I am willful and disobedient and need to prove I can serve."

He threw his head back and stared at the ceiling. "Cameron profiled you."

"He really didn't want me to come." I rested my hand on his firm bicep. "I think you have it all wrong."

"And yet you are here? He does know you well."

"I must complete my training. Please help me."

He rose from the bed and walked across the room to the window, where he stood staring out. "Cameron wants you to have my name in your mouth for the rest of your life." He turned to look back at me. "The question is, do you?"

Footfalls sounded on the stairwell and I knew they were coming for me.

"Scarlet, it's quite possible that I'll be the last master you'll ever have."

How hard could a sub be pushed before she risked her own life?

I heard a knock at the door, and I reached out and clutched the duvet.

"Danton?" A man's voice called out from the hallway.

"We'll be right down," he called back.

I twisted around to look at Danton. "Stay with me, won't you?"

His gaze broke away from mine and he let out the softest sigh. "It's time."

My life was never going to be the same again. "What will happen?"

"Everything changes," he whispered.

"Master, tell them to be gentle with me."

"They're never gentle."

I rose to my feet unsteadily.

CHAPTER 9

France

DANTON CAME OVER AND TIPPED UP MY CHIN. "HAVE YOU
ever climbed through a window?"

"Yes, that's how I broke into D'envoûtement," I said.

He looked amused. "I'm going to have so much fun fucking the crazy out of you."

I pouted at him. "Can't we just walk out?"

"They'll never let you leave." He shook his head, then took off his black jacket and slipped it on me. "They'll fight to keep you. I'm not in the mood to get punched in the face."

Together we hurried over to the window and I watched him slide it up all the way. In what felt like the biggest adventure of my life, we climbed out carefully and made our way along the slanted roof.

We approached the edge and Danton reached out to protect me. "I'll go first."

I turned away from the sheer drop, questioning our sanity, and was hit with a wave of dizziness.

"I can't."

"What did you think this was?" he snapped. "This place?"

"An elite training house for subs?" I raised my gaze to the garden and saw just how tall the wall was that surrounded the estate. This place was a fortress.

"This is the house of Hillenbrand," he said, his tone sounding tense.

"I know that."

"You have no idea what goes on here."

"Cameron warned me they might pierce my clit."

He shook his head solemnly—and proceeded to climb down.

I followed cautiously, clinging to the wood lattice, shoving aside ivy leaves to improve my grip as I slowly descended.

Don't look down. And don't fucking fall.

My descent felt like it took forever. Danton's jacket slipped off my shoulders and I didn't dare look down to see where it had landed. Leaves and latticework dug into my palms as I slid my feet into the small square inlets of the crisscross design.

Danton was waiting at the bottom. He reached up and wrapped his hands around my waist, lifting me the rest of the way down.

I almost fainted with relief when my feet touched the ground.

He pulled me into a hug. "No noise, understand?"

He scooped his jacket up off the ground and swung it back onto my shoulders. I was grateful for it.

With my hand in his, we ran around the left side of the house and soon made it to the front. An hour ago, I'd been crawling along this gravel ground having no idea I'd be exiting so soon.

Everything felt wrong.

I pulled my hand from his suddenly, wondering if Danton was the real threat. How would I even know? I'd not spoken with the other men—they had merely leered at me like predators.

"What's wrong?" he asked.

"I'm scared."

He cupped my face in his hands and pressed his lips to mine, kissing me tenderly.

"I won't let them catch you," he said. "You've got to trust me."

My choices were limited. Go back and be thrown to the wolves, or leave with Danton—not really knowing what kind of man I'd be handing myself over to.

My gut told me to trust him.

I gave a nod to let him know I was ready to continue.

We made our way behind the long line of parked flashy cars. Danton opened the passenger door to a black Lamborghini and ushered me in, then he ran around to the driver's side. He retrieved his key from behind the sun visor and placed it in the ignition.

"If we leave there will never be any chance of your return. You need to understand this. I need you to be sure this is what you want."

"What about you?"

Danton offered me a sad smile. "This was going to be my last evening here."

"Why?"

He stared down at his hands. "Life has other plans for me."

"In what way?"

"You ask a lot of questions for a sub."

"I want to know more about you."

He let out a long sigh.

"I promise to make you happy."

Danton turned to look at me. "You are a gift like no other."

"Where will we go?"

"My family *chateau*. No one will know we're there."

"Danton, I want this more than anything."

He turned the key in the ignition and we took off toward a large closed wooden gate. The car idled before it.

I spun round and gasped at the sight of the men pouring out of the front door, running toward us. I snapped my head back to look at Danton.

He calmly watched them in the rearview mirror.

When the gate opened, he accelerated through it and I was shoved back into my seat as we sped to freedom.

I glanced back to see the men slowing down and ending their sprint toward us.

We drove fast beneath a canopy of trees and within minutes we were speeding along a wide open road.

Danton glanced over at me and reached for my hand, easily driving with his left hand on the wheel. I lowered my window and felt the late night breeze brushing over my face. I breathed in the scented air, my hair becoming a tangled mess.

Jetlag caught up with me and I fell in and out of sleep.

When I awoke, we were driving along a coastal road with an ocean to our left. The moon's reflection danced off its surface. This sense of peace was nothing like I'd ever experienced before, a calmness drawn from Danton's kindness. I couldn't imagine why De Sade would think him cruel. Perhaps that answer lay ahead—and I also knew in my heart I could cope with whatever came my way.

I was a survivor.

I could escape this man, too, if necessary.

All doubt fell away as we pulled up in front of a large *chateau* that sat right on the edge of a cliff. I could hear the sound of waves crashing on a shoreline. The manor was painted in the most exquisite eggshell-blue, and had large, tall windows and a pretty courtyard strewn with multicolored flowers.

We exited the car and I stretched to wake up my tired limbs.

Danton took my hand and led me toward the cliff. He lifted me into his arms and carried me down a long, winding path.

The sound of the ocean grew louder.

I stretched my neck and saw rolling waves crashing onto the sand. Danton kicked off his shoes and continued to carry me toward the ocean.

When we reached the water's edge he put me down. "I can't wait any longer."

I tried to read his intentions, sensing a barely controlled passion that waited for my response.

"Say yes." His lips curved into a smile.

"Yes."

Crushing his lips to mine, his kiss became frenzied as he pulled his jacket off me and threw it to the sand. He then ripped off my nightdress. He began undressing and I helped, ripping his shirt and popping off buttons. We laughed as we tumbled onto the sand together.

He lay on top of me, and I widened my legs, wrapping them around his waist. My back arched as he thrust inside me, fucking me like a man possessed.

He paused and stared down at me, as though checking to make sure I was okay. "All I could think about was doing this to you. Here."

The edge of a wave lapped at my right side, and I turned my head to glance up at the *chateau* that was soon to become my home.

"Are you all right?" he asked, kindness showing in his eyes.

"Yes."

"You don't mind my roughness?"

"No. I need it."

He grabbed my wrists and held them above my head, pounding me against the sand. My orgasm teetered closer.

I never wanted to leave this place.

Danton grabbed my hair and forced me to stare into his eyes. "Where are you?"

"It's all too perfect."

"You're the greatest gift, Scarlet." He buried his face in my neck. "I never want to let you go."

His words wooed me into a well of happiness. Now was not the time to ask how long I'd be staying here, or how my training would be conducted, or if the dazzling chemistry that led to this sudden addiction for each other would endure a lifetime.

The thrum of pleasure in my sex resonated up into my entire body—every cell, every molecule belonged to him and I felt like I already loved this man.

"Tell me you're mine," he whispered, as he thrust deeper.

I wrapped my arms around his neck. "I am."

This was really happening. Leaving Hillenbrand hadn't changed my destiny.

"I'm going to give you everything you have ever wanted," he said, riding me violently. "But there is always a price."

Price?

But I was too far gone to push him away. Writhing in ecstasy against him, I moaned when I felt his wet heat shoot inside me, sending me higher. We shuddered as we came together.

Afterwards, we clutched each other, panting through our post-fucked state of bliss and not caring that the waves were lapping our sides. We rolled onto our backs and stared up at the night sky. The sound of the crashing surf relaxed me further. Peering up I could see no other houses around, and realized the isolation that surrounded us.

Uneasiness welled in my gut. "What did you mean there's always a price?"

He turned to look at me. "Pain is relative."

"What does that mean?"

"You're still so young. So dreadfully naive."

"I'm not."

He turned his head to look at me. "Had you stayed at Hillenbrand, they would have killed you."

CHAPTER 10

France

HEART POUNDING, I PUSHED MYSELF TO MY FEET.
There were so many conflicting messages coming from Danton. He'd told me Cameron had conspired behind my back to trick me into coming to France—and now this, a warning that the house we'd escaped from was a sinister threat to any subs that entered.

He rose. "It means you're safer with me."

"Explain what that place really is."

And why the hell you were there.

He waved it off. "It's lost in translation. You misunderstood. I meant they would have fucked you night and day back at Hillenbrand. And you've had no anal training, at all."

"They would have had to have caught me first."

"I had no trouble catching you."

I shrugged. "Still."

"There would have been no rest for the wicked." He waggled his eyebrows playfully. "It would have been fun to watch though."

"You don't mean that?"

"I'm making a joke." He looked at me with an offended expression. "English is not my first language."

"And it shows."

"Maybe I'll take you back."

I shoved at him.

"I'm serious," he smirked.

"No, you're not," I said, pointing at him. "You're in just as much trouble as I am. I'm going to have words with De Sade when I see him again." I let Danton take my hand and lead me across the sand. "I didn't once mention to him I had a capture fantasy."

Then I remembered I was in the middle of nowhere with the renowned Monsieur Danton. From the way he was staring at me, he might have been thinking the same thing.

We made our way up the winding path. I tripped and he caught me, lifting me up into his arms.

I hoped I hadn't just run off with a psychopath.

When he smiled, though, there was no malice, no meanness—just an endearing sweetness from a man who obviously worshipped sensual deviance.

Just like me.

Dry leaves crunched beneath his feet. The grandeur of his beautiful home rose into view, a place that no doubt contained a lifetime of memories. From Danton's expression, he might have been haunted by a few; his eyes were filled with melancholy and something else, perhaps thoughts of our future here.

I truly hoped so.

Despite all these uncertainties, and the fact I hardly knew him, we'd connected on a level of trust I'd never before known existed—a connection that went beyond the physical.

He'd seen I needed rescuing and had not thought twice about the consequences.

I loved his sweet smile, the way he touched me, gently at first, and then with a commanding grip that guided me. He was my dark prince who'd whisked me away from my misadventures—my naivety so glaring I cringed when I thought of it.

He unlocked the front door.

Danton carried me over the threshold like a husband carrying his new bride, and it made my heart soar. He moved quickly through the living room and I had glimpses of furniture covered in white dust sheets. This place had been abandoned for a while. It was such a beautiful house, and its location right on the beach made it perfectly fabulous. I couldn't understand why anyone would ever want to be away from here.

"Has this always been your home?" I asked, as he carried me up a staircase.

"I grew up here."

I nuzzled into the crook of his neck. "No one lives here now?"

"We live here. You and me."

It was like a fairy tale, being tucked away in a beautiful *casa* right on the ocean with the man of my dreams.

After we showered in his white-tiled bathroom, I lay sprawled on the deep blue duvet covering his large bed and watched him dress. His physique was carved into a perfect form. He was tall and lean, his movement graceful, his confidence glaring as he pulled on his slacks and white shirt. Each measured gesture of his was hypnotic to watch.

"What do you do for work?" I imagined him being a lawyer or businessman, or having some kind of position where his natural authority would shine.

He grinned at me. "I save naughty subs from getting into trouble. And then I dedicate the rest of my time to fucking some sense into them."

"Seriously." I frowned playfully.

"I am." He turned to the window and pulled back the large, linen curtains.

Dust sparkled in the sunbeams, twinkling around us like tiny stars. He looked so dreamy silhouetted there by the window.

Blinking against the bright rays, I sucked in my breath at the view.

Stretching before us—filling the window frame—was the vista of a dark blue ocean. It could be seen from any angle in the room.

Danton stared out at the seascape. "We'll wake up to this every morning."

"I am in heaven," I whispered.

His expression changed to adoration. "I was just thinking that."

"How can you ever bear to leave this place?"

"I forgot what's important." He gave a nod and gestured for me to join him.

Still naked, I slid off the bed and walked toward him. He wrapped his arms around me and pulled me into a hug.

"You'll stay a while?" he said.

I spun round and stared up at him. "Can I stay forever?"

"If I owned forever it would be yours."

Resting my head against his chest, I nuzzled in, realizing I'd been given the greatest gift of time with him—and so far there'd been no talk of my training, or punishments, or emersion as his slave. We were acting like a lovesick teen couple who couldn't bear to tear their hands off each other.

"You must be exhausted," he said. "You've been up all night."

"You too?"

"These days my sleep is erratic."

"Why?"

"Lately, I've not been sleeping well. It's nothing. I get headaches. So I sit in a dark room and listen to music until they pass." His gaze returned to the ocean.

"Is it allergies?"

He looked thoughtful. "No."

"Cameron showed me this trick for headaches," I said. "You

squeeze between the thumb and index finger really hard…like this." I lifted his hand to show him. "It's acupressure. Works on me every time."

He smiled thoughtfully. "You're close to Cameron?"

"Yes, but he won't take me on as his sub."

"You're too fragile for him."

"I'm not." I narrowed my eyes. "Anyway, if that's true why did he send me to you?"

"Because he knows I'll be your perfect master."

"So you're not as harsh as him?"

"We are considered equals."

"What do you know about me?"

"You mean, who is this girl when she's not offering herself to the house of Hillenbrand?"

I stared up at him.

"I know enough," he said.

"You know I'm a waitress?"

"That you were accepted to study at Harvard. Yes, I know this."

"De Sade told you all about me?"

"He did." Danton lowered his voice as though others could hear. "What he failed to tell me was how young you are and how inexperienced."

"Not *that* inexperienced."

His body stiffened against mine and he held me tighter. "We need to find you some clothes."

Danton led me through the house along sprawling hallways that made me feel like we were in a maze, proving how large the place actually was. He guided me into a bedroom and told me that it had once belonged to his sister. We found a few abandoned clothes hanging in her wardrobe.

He let me choose what I wanted to wear, so I picked out white pants and a loose-fitting blouse with puffy sleeves. Happily, his sister's flip-flops were also a perfect fit. I felt so very bohemian.

Danton approved. He'd looked relaxed as he'd helped me dress.

Yes, this was what he liked, I realized. He enjoyed bathing, dressing, and quite possibly feeding his sub, and I went with it, letting him nurture me like I'd never been cared for before.

This was not how I'd imagined my first evening at the house. I felt so comfortable and completely pampered…and so loved.

The rest of the evening was spent preparing the house. Both of us pulling dust sheets off all the beautiful furniture, opening windows to air the rooms, and I'd been left for a while on my own to explore. I counted at least five bedrooms.

One of them led to a locked door at the very top of the house. I leaned down to peer through the keyhole, but couldn't make anything out.

I continued to explore and soon found the kitchen. It was all white tile and old-fashioned appliances, and yet this decades-old style gave the room a welcoming feel. There was no pretentiousness here, only vintage touches that added to the coziness.

The lack of food proved this place really had been abandoned for quite a while. I found a few bottles of water and finished off one of them—though Danton had told me it was safe to drink from the tap.

Afterward, I stood on the bedroom balcony staring out at the remarkable view. I could smell the scent of jasmine on the breeze.

Danton wrapped his arms around my waist, and I jumped a little, not having heard him approach.

"Where did you go?" I asked.

"I called Cameron."

I turned around in his arms and stared up at him. "Why?"

"I wanted him to know you're safe."

"Was he angry?"

"No." He gave me the sweetest smile.

I studied his face, trying to see what he was thinking.

Danton held my gaze. "If at any time you want him to come and get you, I can arrange that."

"Why would I want that?"

He looked thoughtful. "You might get homesick?"

No, that was not it. There was something in the way he'd broken my gaze, a moment of doubt in his eyes.

"We should drive into town," he said, quickly changing the subject. "We need to shop. We need to cook."

"Will you visit me in America? When all this is over?"

He hesitated and I took that as his answer.

Danton was right, of course. We were a temporary item and something told me that leaving here was going to be challenging for me when the time came.

"I found a room at the top of the house," I said. "Why's it locked?"

"It's a storeroom for antique books. That kind of thing. Nothing of any importance."

"I like antiques."

"And don't go into the garden yet. I want to be the one to show it to you."

"Okay. I can do that. Where's your family?"

"My parents moved to Paris to be closer to their friends. This place was too isolated for them." He walked away from me and gripped the edge of the railing. He paused, looking a little pale.

"Are you hungry?" I asked, moving closer to him. He'd driven all night and all I'd thought about was me.

"We'll have dinner in town." He perked up. "Tomorrow, after you've rested, we'll start your training." He put an arm around my shoulders. "I want us to get to the place where you know me. You feel safe with me. Where you'll do anything I ask of you."

"Do you think the men back at the house will try to find me?"

"They might." He lips curved into a smile. "Aren't you tired?"

"I slept on the flight over." And then it hit me. "I don't even know where we are."

"Le Harve. Come let me show you the town."

We made our way to the front of the house and climbed back into his black Lamborghini. We drove into the pretty village and I was mesmerized by the historical architecture, the foreign looking cars and the quaint stores.

We parked outside a food market and headed on in, holding hands.

"What do you do for a living?" I asked. "I mean really?"

"I once dabbled in music."

"You were in a band?"

He laughed. "Kind of. Hours wasted when I should have been living." He kissed the top of my head. "I'm making up for it now."

"Look—" I grabbed a shopping cart, jumped on the edge and wheeled down the aisle. "We can pretend we're married."

Danton laughed and came after me. He grabbed me around the waist and pulled me off. I waited for him to berate me, but all he did was grin and shake his head. "We can be whatever you want us to be," he said. "Just be happy. That's all I ask of you."

"I am happy here, Danton...truly happy."

He kissed my forehead. "Cameron told me he knew me better than I knew myself. Now, I believe him."

CHAPTER 11

France

NAKED AND ON MY KNEES IN MY SUBMISSIVE'S POSE, I waited for Danton.

He'd sat me here in the center of what looked like an old ballroom, beneath a long line of stunning chandeliers that reminded me of upside-down tulips—mesmerizing to look at.

The house was alive with sunlight. Everything here was breathtaking.

Staring up at the gold and sparkling crystals, I tried to imagine what it might have been like to grow up here. There was so much about Danton I wanted to know.

With the fall semester looming, I pushed all thoughts of my future away and slipped into the zone, rising on my knees to peer over the edge of the window frame and look out at that endless ocean.

I marveled at how Danton had made me feel at ease so quickly, and wondered how our first session would go now.

The door opened and he stood there bare-chested, the muscles of his sun-kissed torso rippling. He looked so handsome wearing a tight pair of leather pants.

He held a horsewhip in his left hand.

Steadily, he came forward, closing the gap between us, strolling confidently, a beautiful vision as the refracted lights from the chandeliers wavered over him.

Danton had a glint of a smile in his eyes.

He placed the whip between my teeth and instructed me to crawl behind him.

On all fours I followed him out of the great hall and onward down a long hallway.

He let me stand when we reached a door that looked like it led outside. A blindfold was placed over my eyes. A set of headphones came down around my ears.

With my senses compromised, this was trust in its purest form.

He removed the whip from between my teeth and led me forward. From the drop in temperature I knew we'd stepped outside. Barefoot, I trod on what felt like grass, the softness a nice cushion beneath my soles.

After several minutes we stopped and there came the faint sound of another door opening, even with the headphones on I could tell the door was lighter on its hinges.

The binding of my wrists was quick and Danton did all this to me in silence. I sucked in breaths knowing the pain would come soon and bracing for it as he secured me with my arms above my head.

Classical music burst into my ears.

I smiled, hearing the disarming notes of a cello. I wished Danton could hear it and enjoy the music, too.

"It's beautiful!" I called out louder than I needed to.

A whip struck my ass and silenced me.

He trailed his warm hand down along my spine and squeezed my bottom. I felt him stalking around me, tweaking my nipples as he prowled, and then cupping my sex with a firm hand. A jolt rushed through me when he ran a fingertip along my clit, flicking it slowly.

Spacing out, I savored the sensations as he teased me relentlessly. I felt the dampness between my thighs, his fingers slick against me, the perfect touch of a renaissance man.

A moan slipped from me when he ceased his play.

The whipping started light on my thighs, and he tapped between them until I rose on my tiptoes to avoid the delicious strikes that stung.

My whole body sang when he touched me.

He twisted his hand in my hair and brought me forward, crushing his lips to mine, his tongue darting into my mouth so tenderly and then devouring me with a passion I'd never experienced before, as though with this kiss he was revealing how he felt about me.

With my arms stretched up and wide, I was powerless to reach out and hold him to me.

And suddenly he ripped himself away.

A strike at my belly told me the session was well underway. At first the stinging of the whip was almost too much to bear, as though his kiss had weakened my resolve. But as my skin came alive and was warmed, I sunk into the rhythm.

Round and around he moved with his ceaseless torture, and I rested my head back and took everything he wanted to give—every pinch, every slap, and every unexpected thrust of a palm to nudge me into a better position.

When he set a pace of spanking my buttocks, I slipped further into subspace and rocked against his palm. Deeper and deeper I went, enjoying the sensation of his hand meeting my sensitized skin, which was surely bright red by now. When he fastened the clamps to my nipples I bit through the discomfort, and then almost came when they worked their magic of stimulating my areolas.

Danton's dark machinations went on forever, or so it felt, and I hung forward in a state of happiness.

He rewarded my obedience.

Still blindfolded, I felt his mouth latch onto my sex, lapping hungrily, his hands cupping my butt and pulling me into him, his tongue darting into me.

In my mind's eye, I knew he was bowing at my feet and it felt like a prelude to how my very own sub might worship me when the time came.

But right now I was still his submissive and I knew better than to climax without permission.

The blissful sensation ceased, and I moaned at this loss of pleasure.

Danton placed what felt like a leather strap around my waist, pulling it taut around my belly and nudging me forward. My legs rose off the ground as though I were flying. Danton slid between my thighs and thrust his cock deep inside me.

He stilled completely.

I wiggled to encourage him to move and a hard slap came down on my butt.

Waiting for him to take me felt like an eternity, my body shuddering as I forced myself to relax, my pussy squeezing his cock in encouragement.

Slowly at first, he began that long glide inside me and then withdrew all the way out. I bit my lip to prevent myself from going crazy and wiggling, trying to fuck him back. This was a test of my ability to let my master continue to lead.

It took all my will to surrender to him.

Finally I relaxed, and his steady pummeling sent me into an erotic trance, like an out of body experience that felt transcendent.

He leaned over and removed the clamps to play with my nipples, and I was so swept away I came, screaming during my orgasm, overwhelmed with bliss and barely hearing myself yell over the music. Out of control, I became a writhing mess as my body swayed back to take all of him in and devour all he had to give as I felt his wet heat shoot into me.

Panting, I felt too exhausted to move in my swing. I just hung there, savoring the sensations of his cock still buried deep inside me and his firm hand trailing along my back.

I moaned when he pulled out of me.

The music ceased and I felt the headphones slip off—yet my blindfold remained.

"Scarlet," said Danton.

"Master." I leaned forward wanting to rest my cheek against his chest.

His hand cupped my face. "Was that nice, my sweet sub?"

"Yes," I said, sounding breathless.

"You respond well."

"Thank you, Master."

"Promise you'll be honest with me."

"Always."

"I want to ask you a question."

"Yes."

"Why do you not value your life?"

I froze, a million thoughts racing through my brain.

Could Cameron have told him? Had they talked that long? Surely he'd not shared my most sacred secret…that dreadful, shameful secret.

My death wish.

"What do you mean?" I shook my head, trying to make the blindfold slip so I could see his face, read his meaning.

"Cameron accepted you into his club for one reason, Scarlet."

"Because he knew I'd make a great submissive."

"Because he saw you in the ER having your stomach pumped. That was before you trespassed into his club."

My thoughts scattered as I realized what Cameron actually knew. "He's lying."

"Don't. Not to me."

"Have I not just proven I'm a good girl?"

"You can't manipulate me, Scarlet. Now talk to me."

"About?"

"Your suicide attempts?"

"That was a misunderstanding."

And why the hell was he bringing that up now? It had nothing to do with anything.

"So, you're not going to open up to me either?"

"Untie me."

"No one knows you're here."

Panic welled inside my breast. "Cameron does."

"He's thousands of miles away." His fingers wrapped around my throat. "I'm going to make it quick."

"What are you doing? Danton!"

"Giving you what you want."

"I don't understand."

"I'm Danton Belfort, the bringer of death. That's why they sent you to me. So that you are put out of your misery."

Shock chilled my bones.

His ironclad grip tightened around my throat. "It's a pity. You're such a pleasure to fuck."

The air rushed out of me. I couldn't think, couldn't fight back. I was drowning in fear.

And I'd been so wrong.

All I wanted now was to live…

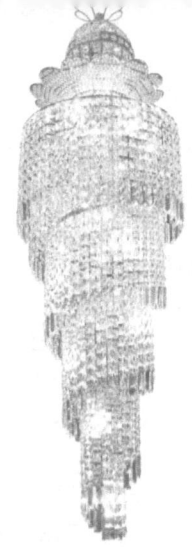

CHAPTER 12

France

HE LOOSENED HIS GRIP.

Relief flooded through me, and I took ragged breaths, trying to refill my lungs.

"Scarlet," he said, his tone softening, "do you like the taste of death?"

"Please," I gasped out.

His hand wrapped around my throat again.

"No, please, Danton! I want to live."

"Admit that's why you came to France. To kill yourself."

"Take off my blindfold!"

His fingers tightened around my neck.

"I…admit it," I stuttered. "I knew Cameron would try to stop me."

He pulled his hand away. "Firstly, I would never hurt you. Deep down you know that. I need you to see the futility of suicide. It changes nothing. All it does is rid us, the ones left behind, of the ones we love. It rids you of an incredible life that's waiting for you on the other side."

"The other side of what?"

"Your pain."

His answer was that simple.

I wiggled in my bindings, wanting to run from my shame. "I won't do it again."

And I meant it. I couldn't do such a thing now, not after finding him...

"We're not done," he said sternly.

Danton was trespassing into my private world and no one had any right to dig around in my thoughts or dredge up these awful feelings.

"I know why you hate yourself," he whispered.

Pain stabbed my heart. *No one knows.*

"This one small final step, Scarlet, let me take it with you."

"What are you going to do?"

"It's you who must determine why you came to France to die."

"To rid myself of the pain," I admitted. "It hurts so bad."

"You never believed I'd be able to ease your pain, did you? Not really?"

I lowered my head, realizing he was trying to help me. "I'm worthless. No one wants me. I'm only here because you felt sorry for me."

I'd been living in foster care all my life, going from one fucked up home to the next, never finding peace.

Until now.

"I love you, Scarlet Winters. And Cameron loves you, and De Sade loves you. You deserve this gift of life. Every breath of it." He pulled me into a hug. "We need you to see what a gift life is. How can you throw away something so precious? We need you."

"I'm not sure you do."

"I know your father hurt you."

Panic struck as I realized he knew about a secret I'd kept hidden for a decade.

"He rejected you. Yet he spoils your half-siblings?" added Danton.

Yes, Dad was a good father to them. I'd gotten the painful

privilege of seeing how he treated them when they'd appeared in the news as an affluent family hailed as New York royalty. My pretty half-sisters, all three of them, often posed at those high-society parties in the latest glamour magazines, all of them out on the town and enjoying their privileged upbringing. They probably didn't even know I existed. How precious they looked to Dad in photos where they all huddled as one big happy family to prove theirs was a dynasty like no other.

"I'm forbidden from contacting my dad," I said, sobbing.

"Your mother was his mistress?"

Cameron had known this all along, though I'd never realized it until now. He'd told Danton my dirty little secret. I was more than the black sheep of the family—I was the daughter that never was.

"Daniel H. Rosenberger." Danton said my father's name so I wouldn't have to.

He seemed to know everything; that I was the lovechild of a fast-rising presidential candidate, a man of wealth and status, who just happened to get his mistress pregnant. Her lovechild was quickly stashed away where no one could ever learn of the scandal that would bring down an empire. They buried me in the fostering system.

My birthright was my shame.

"I'm not allowed to talk about it," I whispered. "Men from my dad's work visited me when I tried to connect with him. They told me it wouldn't end well if I contacted him again. He doesn't want to see me."

"You threaten his clean-cut image, his aspiration of becoming president of the United States."

"Yes."

"You've never known the love of a father?"

I shook my head, trying to rid myself of the memories of all those places I'd lived, where the desire to survive was more important than the need for affection.

I'd been thrown away like trash.

Tears stung my eyes and I felt myself being lowered to the ground.

"This is your worth," he said. "I've never loved anyone like I love you."

"We hardly know each other."

"True. But I love you. And I want to spend every moment with you. I need you to feel what true adoration is. Will you let me show you?"

"You really believe I'm worth it?"

"God, yes."

He planted kiss after kiss upon my lips, his tongue slipping inside my mouth to do battle, but I let him win this war because somehow, some way, he was proving I belonged. For the first time in my life I knew what it was to be immersed in the kind of serenity I'd only yearned for until now.

The blindfold was tugged from my eyes.

Blinking, my vision blurry at first, I took in the enormous glasshouse filled with lush foliage.

Butterflies fluttered around everywhere. As my gaze adjusted, I peered at the ceiling, wide open to the sky, which proved they chose to be in here. They could easily fly away.

I gasped at the mesmerizing vision.

A blue and yellow butterfly landed on my shoulder and I laughed.

"Promise me you won't try to take your life again." He brushed a strand of hair away from my face.

I stared into Danton's eyes and smiled to reassure him that life meant more to me now, and I wanted so much for him to believe that. "I promise."

A butterfly landed on his nose. He gave me a sweet smile, and laughed as it flew away. "I have a secret, too."

"What is it?" I tipped my chin to meet his kiss and melted as his mouth brushed over mine.

He smiled against my lips. "I'm waiting for you to fall for me first."

I leaned my head against his chest and sighed.

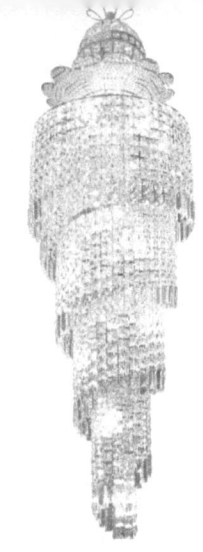

CHAPTER 13

France

I N THE PALM OF MY HAND I CARRIED THE DELICATE TWISTED seashell back to Danton, my toes sinking into the warm sand. I'd just retrieved it from the ocean bed and it was the prettiest one yet.

After removing my snorkel I held it out for him. "Look at this one." I placed the shell into his free hand and sat down on the blanket beside him, pulling a bottle of orange juice out of our picnic basket.

"Want one?" I asked.

"Just drank some." He put his novel down. "Good find, Scarlet." He swept a towel up and wrapped it around my shoulders to keep me warm.

"I'm going to find a jar and put them all in there. I'll collect shells from every beach we visit in the world and keep them as memories."

He carefully laid the shell next to me.

"Do you collect anything?" I asked softly.

"Swim with me?" He gazed toward the water. "Let's have fun in the ocean."

I leaped to my feet and he chased after me, both of us splashing and laughing as we dived in. We crashed into each other and I wrapped my legs around his waist and held on tight, the small waves edging us on.

We made love right there in the sea, his body warming mine, his caresses carrying me away into a bliss I'd grown accustomed to.

I had always loved him.

That's how it felt to be around Danton because he was so incredibly kind and generous in every conceivable way. His enduring strength was always balanced by his boyish sweetness.

Whenever I took a shower, he'd lean on the doorjamb just staring at me with a smile that reached his eyes, before climbing in to join me. Or I'd raise my gaze from a book I was reading and see him staring as though he were trying to take a mental photograph of me.

Since that first BDSM session in the greenhouse three days ago, we'd never mentioned my ominous past again. We didn't need to. I'd felt as though all those feelings of inadequacy had fallen away and now I was validated.

We were inseparable.

After our daily swim, we'd freshen up and cook dinner together. He'd teach me a new recipe and I was his eager student. He talked endlessly about his childhood and the loneliness he'd sometimes felt being the only son. His sister was estranged from the family, he told me. We really were meant for each other.

As the weeks passed, he seemed determined to educate me in all manner of subjects. We'd settle in the sitting room with a roaring fire and sip brandy and talk about everything from politics to art and even music, which he knew so much about.

During those long evenings he'd even try to teach me how to play chess—like tonight, with the air so still and the moon hanging low in the sky.

He moved his bishop and knocked off mine. "I wish we had more time."

"We have all the time in the world."

"You have university to attend."

"Maybe I won't go."

"That's not an option. Education is everything."

"I don't want to leave you."

He waved that off. "Life is like a game of chess. One should be unpredictable, but keep things simple, all the while observing patterns. Always try to think wisely, and always be kind even when the world treats you unfairly."

I rested my hands in my lap.

"Scarlet?"

I slipped out of my pleasant daydream, realizing he'd never once mentioned visiting me in the States.

Danton pointed, indicating I should move my chess piece across the board. "Where were you just now?"

"This game is too hard." I threw my piece down. "I'm too stupid to learn it."

"You got into Harvard."

"That was a fluke."

"You don't really believe that? Now, tell me what's really bothering you."

"I'm not sure I want to go back. Can I stay with you?"

"No, you have so much to give this world. Have you not been listening to anything I've been telling you?"

I stared at him. "Why do you never talk about visiting me when I leave?"

"Go and stand in the corner," he ordered. "Face the wall."

I did as I was told. When he'd seen no remorse in me, he'd bent me over his knee and lavished an exquisite spanking, his left hand meeting my buttocks in painful strikes and his right hand fingering my clit at the same time. I'd pumped my hips furiously against his hand as I moaned through my release.

Afterward, trembling and sated, I knelt before him on the floor and waited for his next order, my head resting on his knee and feeling safe. He made me sit there obediently as he read the newspaper from cover to cover, his left hand trailing through my locks and making my scalp tingle.

The crackling of the fireplace was the only noise; the delicious scent of burning wood reminding me of the Christmases I'd never had.

I wished we could stay in this house forever.

My most favorite time was when we visited his library. It was a cozy room stacked with wall-to-wall books and decked out in leather armchairs and mismatched rugs, with the lingering scent of stale cigars reminding us of the past. I watched him bring down from the shelves several of his favorite philosophy books. Together we carried them down to the beach for our daily picnic by the sea.

In between munching on our sandwiches and sipping freshly squeezed orange juice, he read from his books and I'd swim and collect more shells.

Today, like every day, when he found a passage in his book he liked he would share it with me.

His obsession with history always made me smile.

I'd lay my head on Danton's stomach as he relayed what he knew about Epicures' writings, an ancient Greek philosopher who believed that one should treat others justly, and who had stressed the importance of pleasing oneself and taking proper care of one's body. Danton would beam with happiness when he taught me about Aristotle, a man who encouraged doing good—not just being good.

It felt like I was being groomed for the world.

For the first time I knew I was loved entirely—and all the attention I'd craved as a child and had been denied was lavished upon me now.

We made sure the books were safe in our picnic basket, and then we walked the full length of the beach to discuss what he'd taught me.

I'd never known true happiness until now.

CHAPTER 14

France

MY HAND REACHED OUT FOR DANTON BUT ALL I FELT was a cold bedsheet.

Rain struck the windowpane and it made me feel so warm and snug in our large bed. I sat up and stretched, checking the bedside clock. It was just after midnight.

A flash of lightning scared the hell out of me and I leaped out and went to look for Danton.

Padding along the hardwood floors, hoping to quickly find him so I could persuade him to return to bed, I was thinking of all the luscious ways I was going to help him fall back to sleep.

A window was open somewhere, letting a draft in. I realized it was coming from Danton's office.

When I nudged open the door, I saw him sitting in his corner armchair, bare-chested and dressed only in his pajama pants, which were pulled down off his hips. A needle was injected into his left thigh and his expression looked tense with concentration. A flicker of pain crossed his face.

My gaze caught an empty ampoule on his desk. I walked forward and reached for it. Danton's eyes rose to meet mine and he watched me pick up the glass vial.

Morphine.

I dropped it onto the desk and flew out of there, running through the house, my heart pounding, my head full of confusion.

I couldn't breathe.

"Scarlet," he called after me.

I burst through the front door and bolted down the pathway, almost tripping on the rocks and grass and sticks that dug into my soles, not caring about the rain soaking my nightdress, having no thought of where I'd end up.

I sprinted onwards toward the crashing waves.

All this time Danton had feigned he was a man of the highest integrity, and he'd expected so very much from me—demanding the same, demanding honesty. I felt so damn stupid as I realized all the signs had been there: those moments when his drug intoxication had worn off and he'd gone pale and acted a little moody, only to disappear to be alone for a while *again*.

To give himself his fix.

On so many afternoons Danton had insisted we take a nap to recuperate, even on those lazy days we'd just spent basking in the sun.

Now it all made sense.

My feet carried me across the sand toward the water. Waves lapped at my feet as a stark chill soaked into my bones.

"Scarlet!" Danton's voice rose above the crashing surf. "Scarlet, please."

"Go away!"

"It's not what you think," he said, approaching me.

"Morphine?"

"Yes, but—"

"How long? How long have you been an addict?"

He leaned over and rested his hands on his knees. "I didn't want you to find out like this." He tried to smile. "Give me a second."

"I hate you." I spat out. "You act all high and mighty. Expecting so much of me—"

"Please let me explain." Danton straightened to his full height. He faced the ocean and shook his head.

We were both soaked from the rain; him with his pants sticking to his legs and me with my nightdress clinging to my cold flesh.

"You can't stay out here." He could see I was shivering in the unrelenting downpour.

I backed away from him in protest.

My hair was plastered to my head. I brushed a clump of locks away from my face. "How could you?"

"Think, Scarlet. That's what I've taught you to do. Put all the pieces together."

"You're using it for your headaches? That's ridiculous."

"Sweet butterfly, come here." He looked worn down, his face even paler.

"Morphine for headaches?" I snapped.

"The cause of the headaches."

My throat felt dry with grief.

He caressed his temple. "I was waiting for the right time to tell you. You were just so happy. So many times I started to say it and…"

"What?"

He stared at me, his expression strained with pain.

I froze with fear. "What's wrong with you?"

"If only I could find a way to make it go away."

Words refused to form in my mouth.

He gave a shrug. "I have a brain tumor."

No. This wasn't happening. I'd just found him.

"I don't believe it. Tell me the truth."

"Oh, Scarlet. I'm so sorry."

"How long have you known?"

He swept back strands of his dripping wet hair. "A year."

"You should have told me."

"I meant to. I was terrified it would ruin what we had, taint our days and nights that have been so perfect, that have helped me forget."

All the pieces came together like a puzzle solidifying in my mind. "Hillenbrand?"

"It was meant to be my final visit there. A little indulgence before I had to give the lifestyle up. Then I saw you, realized you had no idea about the other doms. I couldn't leave you there. They would have devoured you. Cameron sent you to me knowing full well I'd get you the fuck out of there and probably take you home with me."

"He didn't want you to be alone here?"

He looked away, devastated. "It was selfish to make you mine."

"Cameron and De Sade knew all along?"

"I'd told them both months ago that I was planning on coming home to die…alone. Told them I just wanted to go quietly with no fuss." He let out a deep sigh. "They asked me for one final favor, to meet you at the airport. See their new submissive safely to the house. I could play a little with you for a few hours, they told me. Fuck a little…if you wanted that."

I shook my head trying to comprehend their scheming.

"I was manipulated." Danton sucked in a gulp of air. "When you turned up at the airport you were brave and strong and full of life. You were beautiful. They knew I'd crave you. Feel your vitality and not be able to live without it. Without you."

"I love you," I stuttered out. "I need you. There must be a cure?" I ran to him and wrapped my arms around his waist.

"There's nothing to be done."

I looked up at him realizing he'd brought me here for two reasons: to save me and to keep from having to die alone.

"I want to give you every part of me, Scarlet. Show you that life is good. I saw your pain, saw what life had done to you and I knew I could help you, too. When Cameron told me you'd tried to kill yourself it broke my heart. And here I was fighting for my life. I thought if I could just make you see that life is a gift."

Tears stung my eyes and my heart was flooded with pain at the thought that Danton couldn't be mine forever.

"Forgive me for doing this to you." He hugged me tighter.

"Cameron knew we needed each other."

"He's an interfering bastard." He pulled me back toward the pathway. "You'll catch a cold out here. Please, let's go back to the house."

"Danton? How long do you have before…?"

"A month, perhaps."

No! This was a nightmare. It didn't seem real.

But I saw the proof. Here he was, taking a moment to pause and catch his breath halfway up the hill, his expression strained, knowing he had the rest of the way to go before we reached the house.

He needed me.

Not a selfish, immature girl, but a woman who deserved him, my Danton. A lover who understood why he'd once planned on dying alone. The thought of him facing this ordeal in solitude was too terrible to bear.

All this time I'd believed it was him saving me, but now I knew I was meant to be here for him.

But I knew I'd never survive losing him.

Surely Cameron and De Sade had thought of that? Their scheming would lead to a kind of pain a woman would never recover from.

I remembered what Danton had once said to me.

"Cameron wants you to have my name in your mouth for the rest of your life. The question is, do you?"

Yes, I silently screamed. I want this more than anything.

Before Danton I'd hated my life, tasted only bitterness, never once dared to believe that this world might one day find a place for me in it. Death had always seemed so inviting, an enticing doorway through which I'd escape my despair.

But here, now, my love was about to be snatched up in Death's arms. I hated how I'd been so willing to throw away something so pure when he was fighting for his life.

Cameron had known all along that I needed to face death and be around it to truly understand it.

I forced back my tears, trying to be strong for him. My breathing became ragged from the pressure of holding back this tidal wave of grief.

Danton wasn't fooled.

"I'm not dead yet, silly." He reached out to grab my hand. "Come on." He led me toward the house. "I want to savor each moment with you. Promise me you'll be strong for me."

I loved him too much to ever leave him and this was my chance to prove how much I adored him. I'd wait until he slept soundly before I shed any tears. I would hide from him all my worry and be everything he needed me to be, give him everything he wanted in his final weeks.

Once inside we stripped off our soaking wet clothes and dried ourselves off in the bathroom.

Thunder clapped just outside the window and lightning flooded the room, and we ran into the bedroom as though we could hide from it. Danton was laughing, as though he felt relieved that his secret was out.

How could he be this strong? So brave and willing to face the most dreadful of curses?

He threw himself onto the bed and forced a smile. "Scarlet, let me love you."

I leaned low and took him into my mouth. He grew hard instantly. Sucking, I let out a moan of relief that he was still mine.

Then I felt a sudden rush of despair. I pulled away from him.

"Shush," he soothed, his fingers playing with my hair.

I forced back a sob. "We're going to find a cure."

"Less talking," he said with a grin. "More sucking."

After taking him all the way to the back of my throat as far as I could go, I worshiped him with licks and kisses, feverishly proving he was everything to me.

He rolled me onto my back and lowered himself between my legs. "Maybe this is where I'll find the magic elixir."

"Don't joke about this."

I'd never survive losing him. My teeth bit into my lip to prevent another sob from escaping as tears stung my eyes.

"See—" He licked along my clit. "I'll live forever in your heart now."

"Yes, forever in my heart."

His tongue flicked faster and I arched my back in pleasure, marveling at how he could draw such strength from someone like me.

Danton pushed himself up. "I'm tying you down. You deserve it."

I let him secure me to the four corners of the bed with red rope. He took his time as though it were some luscious ritual.

Spread-eagled, I felt powerless. When Danton began the slow journey of kissing my feet and then working his way up my body I swooned with delight.

With each second, I brought myself back to a place of strength, where I reassured myself I had everything it took to be there for this wonderful man.

I raised my head off the pillow. "My nose is itchy."

He gave a smirk and reached up and scratched it.

"Other side." I moved my head to the left.

"How's that?" He ran his fingertip over my nose.

"Better."

He kissed my stomach.

"Oh, no," I said.

"What now?"

"I need to pee."

"Now?"

"Yes, now. You have to untie me."

"Do you have any idea how long it took me to tie you up?"

"I was here, remember."

He rolled his eyes playfully and got to work releasing me. I shifted off the bed and padded into the bathroom.

I sat on the toilet and Danton came in and leaned back against the sink.

"Look at us." I beamed up at him. "We're like an old married couple."

Then a dreadful sadness swept over me. Danton seemed to notice, and he gave me a comforting smile.

"Come back to bed," he said. "I want to show you how obsessed I am."

"We're perfect together, aren't we?" I washed my hands beneath the faucet.

He came closer. "We're everything we both need and more."

"I'm scared." I couldn't let the words stay inside me anymore.

He wrapped his arms around my waist and hugged me. "I'm going to give you enough love to last a lifetime."

I stared at his reflection in the mirror. "You already have."

CHAPTER 15

France

T HAT ROOM AT THE TOP OF THE HOUSE HAD CALLED TO ME again.

As though some part of me knew there was something in there significant to Danton's life…his past.

I'd broached the subject of the room one more time and Danton had closed down my line of questioning by quickly changing the subject—and then spanking me deliciously.

I'd lived here for a month now. Surely such time spent with a man and the intimacy we shared warranted no further secrets between us?

Since the day he'd told me to forget that room even existed, I'd mulled over what might be in there. Danton had said it was merely old books, but from the way he'd broken my gaze I knew there was something he was hiding.

I'd tried to forget about it.

Yet the more I forced my thoughts away the more my intrigue grew. Survival was all about following your instincts. Now was the time to shed light on Danton's other secret.

With him resting soundly in our bed—he was sleeping later in the mornings these days—I went off to explore.

In the kitchen was an old bunch of keys I'd found when I'd been busy cooking for us one evening, searching the drawers looking for a can opener for a tin of tomatoes. I'd made a mental note to come back for those keys when I was feeling brave.

I carried them to the upper hallway and tried each one in the keyhole of the mysterious door, my imagination running wild with what I was going to find.

I squealed with delight when one of the keys turned in the lock. I shoved open the door.

It was so beautiful it took my breath away. There on a stand sat the most gorgeous amber-colored cello.

Had the music Danton played to me in the greenhouse come from this very instrument?

Reverently, I stepped toward it, and then saw the musical scores in a neat pile on a table at the back of the room. A few antique books were stacked on a shelf to help validate his previous assertion. I moved closer to the cello, my fingers trailing down the strings. I gave one a tweak and it vibrated in a deep base.

"What are you doing?" Danton asked sternly. He was leaning against the doorjamb.

"Can you play this?"

He gestured for me to come to him.

"That music you played me in the greenhouse, did it come from this?"

"Yes."

That meant he'd recorded a piece of music at some point, confirming just how brilliant a musician he was.

I was astounded. "You really are a cellist?"

"I used to be."

"Why hide it away?" I went to grasp the neck of the instrument and then pulled away, realizing this was something very, very special.

He walked into the room.

"I figured I was going to have to stop at some point," he answered, shrugging.

"That doesn't make any sense."

"It's like—" He placed his hand on his heart. "When you need something so much and you know you're going to lose it. Why bother to fight? Let it go."

"We have each other." I ran toward him and wrapped my arms around his waist. "We're proving that every single moment must be savored. Not one second wasted." I peered up at him. "Aren't we?"

"I have you."

"Play for me."

He waved a hand in the air dismissively.

I pulled away from him and sat on the floor, crossing my legs. "I'm not moving until you play for me."

"You're so very stubborn, Scarlet," he said, grinning. "Let's have some tea. Go make me breakfast, you submissive, you."

"No."

"Come on. This is futile."

"This is you." I pointed to the cello. "This is who you are and you promised me every part of you." I threw my hands up. "I thought you were in a band. You made me believe you were. I imagined you with spiked hair and tight leopard skin pants, playing the guitar terribly on a bad cover you'd recorded with your friends."

"It was easier for me to let you think that rather than explain this."

"This? This is incredible."

He pointed to the cello. "It was once my great love. Now you are."

"I'm not moving, Danton."

"Then you'll gather dust."

"Danton! Get your ass in that chair. *Now.*"

"Ah, my sweet butterfly has stretched her wings and is now a dominatrix."

I crossed my arms.

"Okay." He raised his hands in surrender. "Once. Only because it's you asking."

Cheering, I pushed myself up and fetched a chair for him. Within minutes he'd dusted off the cello and sat with the instrument between his legs, the bow poised in his right hand.

A smile lit up his face. "It's a good thing you're already addicted to me."

Those words couldn't have been truer.

With my heart soaring, I watched, mesmerized, as he swept the bow over the strings masterfully, an elegant movement that proved he was one with the instrument. He made it look so easy. The way he brought the cello to life was the most incredible thing I'd ever seen or heard, musical ribbons flowing in and out continuously in strands of beauty as though light itself was morphing into notes, reaching every corner of the house.

His eyes remained closed as he played U2's "With or Without You"—and seeing his expression, I understood Danton's fear of losing this precious gift. It was like a profound affair between a man and his instrument. His music was utterly breathtaking.

As he brushed the strings with his bow, his face looked just as serene as when he was sleeping.

He suddenly grinned as though he could sense my reaction.

Swept away, awestruck, it was impossible not to let my tears fall.

Every evening, from that moment on, I'd curl up on our bed while Danton sat in a chair near the balcony and played his cello for me.

For me.

CHAPTER 16

France

THE LIMO PICKED US UP AT 6:00 A.M. AND WE HEADED ALONG
the coastline.

Still sleepy from rising so early, snuggling against
Danton's side in the back of the car, my thoughts continued to cycle
around to his illness. Somehow, someway, I knew we'd get through
this.

I prayed we'd find a cure.

He stared out at the passing scenery with his usual sereneness
and control. His hair was parted and a little messy, a dash of carefree
artiness. He'd dressed in a black tailored Armani suit, and he looked as
gorgeously intimidating as the first day I'd met him, with that five-o-
clock shadow enhancing his confident edge.

He was always so dignified.

Before we'd left home, he'd stood me in the middle of the bedroom and dressed me, tugging a little black dress over my body and
then easing on my new knee-high leather boots. All my outfits he'd
had especially delivered to the house.

I'd styled my hair just how he liked it—long and sleek, my bangs straight across my forehead to highlight my blue eyes.

After sharing his devastating news a week ago, he'd carried on as though nothing had changed at all, and I suppose for him nothing had. My own world was in disarray, my emotions swirling like that stormy ocean to our right, the waves crashing onto the rocky shoreline as though reflecting the anger I felt, the unfairness of it all.

Why had life done this to me now? I'd just found my soul mate, only to have him ripped away from me. Life continued to show its cruelest hand. Still, I was going to stay. I wanted to be with him during this ordeal and nothing could stop me.

"I'll go with you," I whispered.

Danton shook his head as though rising from a trance, and then he smiled, his eyes crinkling.

"When you go in for your treatment," I clarified. "I'll be with you at the hospital."

He gave me a sympathetic look.

Searching his face, I tried to fathom what he was thinking. His face wore that usual beautiful expression of serenity.

He stared out the window. "Aren't you curious where we're going?"

I followed his gaze. "Are we going out for breakfast?"

"Where would you choose to go above all?"

"Paris?"

Danton's head fell back in a laugh. "*Oui.*"

"For the day?"

"Yes."

I collapsed against him, planting kisses on his cheek. Our mouths met lusciously, our tongues tangling.

When I'd first arrived in France, that's where I'd thought I'd be living. I'd had no idea I would be whisked away to an ocean side home, where I would be loved so deeply.

We smooched in the back of the car for the entire way, hugging and kissing and making each other laugh. The excitement of knowing

I would finally see the City of Lights made me giddy. With Danton having grown up here, he'd know the best places to visit.

The Louvre was our first stop.

The museum was breathtakingly beautiful, and it went on forever. Of course, Danton knew everything about it, sharing that it had once been a fortress, and now housed some of the most famous paintings in the world.

We bypassed the long line of tourists waiting to get in and entered through a secret door at the side, where we were met by a senior curator who was expecting us. Danton chatted with him a while and it turned out this man was an old school friend. Pierre offered to take us on a tour, but understood when Danton declined and told him we'd find our own way.

We walked through the long hallways and sprawling galleries, and I was mesmerized by the surrounding marble and ceiling murals—the ones framed in gold were hypnotically beautiful.

I had to grip Danton's arm so I wouldn't trip because I was looking up so much.

We finally made it to the painting Danton wanted to show me, the *Mona Lisa*. Slowly nudging our way through the crowd, we managed to get close enough to view her properly. The portrait was smaller than I'd imagined it to be.

Still, she was quite enthralling.

We continued on, stopping now and again to admire a sculpture or take in the brilliance of a painting, some of which were enormous.

Danton knew so much about art and history and sculptures. I clung to him in awe, realizing he was a renaissance man. It seemed there was nothing he didn't know something about. He was like a French Cameron in so many ways. He was kind and generous and brilliant and always willing to share everything he knew about the world.

We settled in the museum café and Danton ordered us two espressos and a croissant each. I had fun watching him people watch and then hearing him share his remarkable observations about the other diners, his wisdom all garnered from a glance, spoken with understanding.

We sat close so we could hold hands, and to those around us we must have appeared love struck. In between kisses, Danton fed me pieces of croissant.

He nurtured me so.

The car picked us up an hour later and we went on to Notre Dame Cathedral. We rested for a long while in one of the pews, listening to psalms sung by angelic choirboys, their singing ethereal as it echoed around us. I couldn't break my gaze from the central stained glass window with its intricate design and vivid colors.

Our next stop was the Eiffel Tower.

The elevator ride to the top of the wrought iron lattice tower was exhilarating. We rose at a constant speed through the metal structure and the view of the city became more impressive the higher we went.

We swapped to a second elevator so we could go all the way to the top, and just like the first it creaked and rattled during its ascent, reminding us just how old the structure was. Danton whispered in my ear that it had been intended to be built in Barcelona, but in the end it had been too expensive for the government. He also told me that the engineer, Gustave Eiffel, had also contributed his knowledge to the design of the Statue of Liberty.

Stepping out of the elevator we made our way to the edge, which was guarded by crisscross fencing that was easy to see through. As I tried to fathom being this high, my breath caught at the spectacular panoramic view of an ancient city fused with modern, glorious architecture, a sprawling metropolis that went on forever.

Strong hands wrapped around my waist and Danton hugged me to him.

"Scarlet," he began softly, "I want you to see how beautiful this world can be. I want you to be conscious and interact with architecture, the arts, with travel and the people you meet. Be the grandest adventurer for me."

I spun round in his arms realizing what he was saying. He wanted to give me every part of himself and all he knew so that when he left me I'd survive. No, more than survive. I'd savor this world as much as he had.

He hugged me tighter. "Promise you'll seize every opportunity."

"I promise."

Danton kissed me tenderly. "Let's stop off in the café for a drink, yes?"

We spent the rest of the afternoon talking and sipping hot tea and Danton shared memories of his childhood. He went on to tell me about his days studying at the Conservatoire de Paris, where he learned to play his beloved cello. I opened up to him about my own childhood in West Virginia, and then the move to Massachusetts, where I'd later met Cameron.

All the sadness that had gone before no longer stung as it once had. Danton had healed my pain and completed me in ways I only now understood.

I felt forever indebted to him.

Our limo picked us up just after 5:00 P.M. and we journeyed through the winding streets, onward to our next adventure.

The car pulled up to the curb in front of a large manor, the grandness of all that dark brick and the arched windows barely visible amongst a sweeping landscape of lush green grass and weeping willows.

Danton gave an order for the driver to return after midnight.

Our chauffeur agreed with a nod.

My thoughts swirled with guesses at what might lay ahead, and noticing his intense expression I wondered if this might be a family visit.

Hand-in-hand, we strolled up the pathway towards the property and I glanced at Danton to gauge his changing mood.

No, this place did not belong to a relative. It belonged to Mistress Delour, or at least she managed this house. She stood at the front door, that beautiful, chic dominatrix with her high cheekbones, looking so regal beneath the soft lighting. Her beauty was hypnotizing and impossible to forget. I remembered her from the car that had picked me up from the airport with Danton. She looked even more stunning now in a black leather bodice that was laced tight around her small waist, its elegant design pushing her breasts up into voluptuous curves.

She gestured for us to enter.

I flashed a glance at Danton as a thrill raced up my spine. I knew that look of determination on his face, recognized by my master's stance that a scene was imminent.

Trust was expected and resistance had no place in a well-trained submissive's world.

I'd made it all the way to The House of Madame Delour, and my heart skipped a beat at what lay ahead for me. My hand reached for Danton's, trying to convey I didn't want him to leave my side. Surely he knew that? Surely he'd see we'd come too far for there to be any chance of him leaving me to find my own way.

We were led down the longest hallway and into a room with plush plaids and floral designs, a mismatch of décor that worked on a decadent level. The high-backed armchairs and lavish cream rug gave the place a Parisian flair.

Danton was pulled away from me by Madame Delour, and they walked over to a corner to speak more privately.

"Eve," he said. "Thank you for hosting us."

She looked at him with awe. "You left Hillenbrand with her? It's quite the scandal."

He turned and gestured for me to move away toward the window to give them space.

I strained to hear them, all the while pretending I couldn't.

"Cameron Cole arranged everything," he whispered.

"I've been worried about you." She cupped his face in her hands.

Her affectionate sadness made me want to turn away, but an un-wavering uneasiness made me continue to eavesdrop.

"Whatever you need, Danton," she said.

"I appreciate that." He sat on the arm of a chair.

She glanced over at me. "As petulant as ever?"

He looked amused.

They continued their conversation in French and I pressed my lips together in frustration.

The garden view was pretty with its colorful flowers. Further down there were high bushes to keep out the voyeurs.

"We've had a full day," Danton finally said in English. "I showed Scarlet the city."

There came a flutter of sadness in my heart that he'd made me part of his goodbye to the city of his birth.

Eve tapped his arm. "Let me order some drinks. Are you hungry?"

"Maybe water."

Their gazes fell on me and I turned and pretended to be interested in the garden again.

Eve lowered her voice to a whisper. "You're leaving her here, aren't you? We'll take good care of her. I promise you that."

Fear slithered up my spine.

CHAPTER 17

France

WHEN THE ACHE IN MY CHEST BURNED TO A FEVER pitch and almost had me falling to my knees, I could take it no more.

I spun round and faced Danton with a glare.

He gave me the kindest smile. "I'd like to ensure our visit goes smoothly."

It was impossible to escape the panic I felt, this roiling well of emotion that had almost crippled me and sparked a wildfire of inner turmoil. Being parted from him was equal to losing the air I breathed. Stepping forward, I gripped the top of a high-backed chair for balance.

"Come here." Danton gestured for me.

Moving quickly, I approached him and sat on the floor, resting my head on his lap, my soul needing this physical contact with him more profoundly than ever.

Danton spoke softly, "Let's see her ambition realized."

Staring up at him, I marveled that he was even thinking of me.

With all we'd done today, along with that heartbreaking revelation that hung like a dark cloud over us, he ignored his own needs and only thought of me.

"Prepare Solene," he said firmly.

Eve smiled. "She'll be happy to see Scarlet again."

He was talking about Eve's submissive, the young woman I'd met in the car and with whom I'd shared the most delectable tryst with Danton.

My spirits rose at the thought of seeing her again. Although we'd not seen each other since that day, we'd enjoyed a sensual connection that had spoken more than words ever could—a submissive bond that went beyond conformity.

Then I realized…

Was I to watch a session with Danton and Solene? My emotions swirled with rising uncertainty.

This…this was why I wanted to dominate and no longer be left out of the decisions that were made on my behalf. Taking control was my destiny—I'd always known that. I'd savored my time as a submissive but always believed there was more for me.

I'd never wanted to be a part of this world more than at this moment.

Eve left us alone to find Solene.

Staring up at Danton in awe at his generosity, I enjoyed the sensation of his fingertips brushing through my locks to calm me, but I was worried for him, too. He had to be tired from our adventures exploring the city.

"We don't have to do this now," I said.

"They sent you to me to be trained by a master. Let's not disappoint."

I pushed myself to my feet and wrapped my arms around his neck. "But I don't want to waste one minute being without you."

"You don't have to."

"You'll be with me?"

He narrowed his gaze. "Yes."

My toes curled in anticipation as that fierce look sent me into subspace, as it had done every time he switched into play. For me it was more than a scene, it was us melding into our authentic selves, two lovers trusting beyond the ordinary and exploring the sensual.

Doubt flashed through my mind.

He seemed to sense this. "Solene is an excellent subject. She is open and obedient." He arched an amused brow as though hinting I could learn a lot from her. He rose to his feet. "Follow my lead, understand?"

"Yes."

"Address me as Master Belfort. You'll present yourself as my assistant dominatrix during the session."

I kissed his cheek, joy rising with the realization he had the power to promote me.

"Come on, we'll go over what is expected from you."

As we strolled through the house I admired the many paintings, lavish light fixtures, sweeping red carpet and elegant décor, and knew we were heading into the very center of an elite society.

His hand tightened around mine and he pulled us faster along the spacious hallway. "You may question why we are doing this now. If I leave you with anything—"

"Don't."

"Let me say it, Scarlet. Life is to be savored. Drink in all you see, quench your thirst on its delights. Have no regrets. It brings me pleasure to make you happy, see you fulfilled."

We made our way down the spiraling staircase, onward down another sprawling hallway until we reached a door.

He pulled a key from his pocket and unlocked it.

We stepped into a lavish room of punishments and pleasures. Long burgundy drapes swept across large windows—and a long chain dangled from the ceiling, along with the dark wooden Saint Andrew's Cross. In the corner sat a spanking bench, and at the far side of the room I saw an elegant velvet chair.

Clothes for us to change into were waiting for us and were already laid out on the bed, proving Danton had planned this visit before we'd even left home this morning. In silence, a kind of reverence I'd only begun to understand, we changed from our formal wear into the attire of Masters of the Dungeon. Danton looked so handsome in his black pants, having no need for a shirt, and he walked around barefoot now, checking the equipment. He looked so at home. I'd been provided with a tight black bodice and a delicate thong. Stunning strappy heels elevated my height to match Danton's.

He pulled me into him, scrunching my hair in a fist, and brought my lips to his in a deep sensuous kiss, his tongue invading my mouth. My eyes closed and I gave a moan of passion. My adoration for him was returned as my tongue tangled with his.

"Now." He became stern again. "Tell me who holds all the power?"

"The submissive." I was breathless from our kiss.

"We have two levels of play, two types of sessions. With a client there will be no intimacy, we merely guide them through the scene professionally. However, with a beloved submissive, where there is an agreement of intimacy, there is the opportunity to lead our sub into a blissful state of sexual arousal and hold them there." He lowered his gaze. "Our pleasure is secondary."

A thrill spiraled up my spine at the knowledge I was about to observe a true master.

The lights were dimmed. The music playing in the background was a classical selection that was not imposing, but helped set the erotic scene.

Eve escorted a crawling Solene into the room. She was naked except for a thong and the fine chains that were wrapped around her breasts and abdomen. Attached to her choker was a long, thin golden chain that Eve tugged on to guide her to the center. Solene looked ethereal, her pale body drenched in a yellow glow of soft light.

Danton soothed her into the scene with whispers of reassurance.

Eve handed the chain to Danton and he ordered Solene to stand.

She rose elegantly, her head slightly bowed, her hands behind her back, her excited gaze flitting back and forth from him to her mistress.

Eve stepped to the back of the room and disappeared into the shadows.

Danton prowled around Solene with a powerful stride. He spoke to her in French, his words poetic, seductive, sensuous…

Another twinge of jealousy stirred within me again, my gut twisting because I had no idea what he was saying to her. My imagination ran wild with how he was going to touch her. The way he was lulling her so seductively made them seem so close, so intimate. She was swooning, her eyelids flickering as she effortlessly slipped into subspace.

No, I couldn't bear to see the man I loved wooing another woman.

"Danton!" My harsh whisper carried over the music.

He turned to face me, his gaze lowered. "Solene, translate what I just told you, please."

"I am to be trained by Mistress Scarlet today." Her eyes rose to meet mine.

Jealousy had made me look foolish again.

Danton turned to face her again and this time spoke in English, "Change of plan, Solene." With a sweep of his hand he summoned Eve. "Another time, perhaps."

Solene bit her bottom lip nervously, realizing it had been me who'd fucked up. She threw me a look of sympathy, which did nothing to soothe my guilt.

They both left the room.

With my head bowed, I waited for the room to cease spinning.

I felt Danton's gaze on me. I looked up and saw no severity in his expression, merely understanding.

"I'm not ready?" I whispered.

"No."

"I should have trusted you."

He gestured for me to walk into the center of the room and stand right where Solene had stood a few moments ago.

"Seeing you with her…" Any explanation felt futile.

He reached up for the long chain dangling above my head and set about securing my wrists within the leather cuffs.

My breathing was ragged now with anticipation at how he was going to respond—with the kind of pain and disappointment I deserved. But as long as he didn't leave me in here with my own thoughts I'd survive this.

Danton strolled around me and his hands worked at the lacing on the back of my corset. He tugged it from me and it fell to the floor. He ripped off my thong, making me jump as the material tore.

Naked and dazed, I pleaded with my eyes.

"You'd have made an exquisite dominatrix." He yanked the chain above my head and raised my arms, forcing me onto my tiptoes. "But you've thrown your chance away."

I tried to find the words to explain.

"There can be no doubt. Your submissive is vulnerable, needful, and you must bend your will to fulfill him or her. There's no room for selfishness."

"Please, give me another chance."

He gave me a roguish smile. "Well, well, what do we have here? A sub in chains."

I'd thrown away the most incredible opportunity to prove I was ready. Now I was dangling from the ceiling, aroused but confused by my lack of judgment.

He studied my expression. "Thoughts?"

"I feel powerless."

"If your ambition is to be a domme so that you hold all the power then you are mistaken. The sub owns the power, they lead the play, and it is a talented domme who senses their yearning and interprets their desires during a session."

"Yes, master."

"Better."

"I want to learn."

He ran his hand through my hair. "Let's start from the beginning."

My toes curled as his fingertips tweaked my nipples.

"Why do we live this life? Some think it's merely an excuse for us to pursue dark, sensual delights and enjoy a decadent existence of glorious fucking. But no, that's not it at all. We embrace life. We accept its sorrows. We relish in the *now*. We worship this gift of sexuality and savor every moment of passion to prove our gratitude. When a sub leaves a dom's side after a session and continues out into the world they are refreshed, reborn, stronger than they ever were before, truly empowered."

Realizing the profoundness of having never let go, I knew that until I surrendered completely I'd never be able to advance in hierarchy.

Danton knelt and leaned toward my sex. He gave me a long, luxurious kiss between my thighs.

Shuddering, pleasure surging through me, I felt his forgiveness as he lapped and cherished me there, suckling and lavishing his endless affection on me to prove he understood.

He broke away and rose to tower over me. "What do I need to do to convince you I adore you? Worship you?" He trailed his finger along my clit. "Does this not show you how well I know your body?"

I moaned as his fingers increased their flicking.

He slapped me there, sending a shock through my body so powerful it equaled a short, sharp climax. "What happens when subs disobey?"

"They get punished," I blurted out. "Punish me, Master."

My heart was thumping rapidly, my gasps causing my breasts to tremble.

Deftly, he freed himself from his pants and lifted me up so that I was able to wrap my thighs around his waist. With one swift movement, he buried himself deep inside me.

My sex clenched around his length as pulses of pleasure sent me reeling. My head fell back, my orgasm snatching my breath away.

Danton's pupils dilated to black, his jaw tense, his concentration focused on delivering aggressive thrusts to show he'd taken back the power. I had no choice but to let him have his way with me.

He slowed the rhythm, and each time he met my sex with an upward strike I let out a scream of pleasure.

This intensity was becoming too much to bear.

He moved his hips in a circle, slowing the pace a little more, trying to keep me from passing out. Again he was proving how merciful he could be with me, how much he respected my need for it just to be *us*.

CHAPTER 18

France

HEART POUNDING, I SEARCHED THE HOUSE FOR DANTON. We'd returned from Paris three days ago and since then he'd been slowly withdrawing from me. Fear that I'd embarrassed him after he'd made such precise arrangements at Madame Delour's haunted me as I ran from room to room.

An hour ago he'd given me *Great Expectations* by Charles Dickens to read and left me in the library, and only now did I suspect it was a diversion tactic as I sprinted out the front door.

With relief, I saw that his car was still parked in the driveway. But the thought of him wandering off along the beach caused me to inhale panic-drenched breaths.

I flew down the garden pathway and let out a sigh of relief when I saw him.

In what looked like a measured frenzy, Danton was dismantling the greenhouse panel by panel, throwing the glass squares down on the grass. He was halfway done with tearing our sacred hideaway apart and it was now unrecognizable.

"I was looking for you everywhere," I said, breathing hard.

He eased apart another panel and it cracked down the center.

"Look what you've done now," he snapped. "You're a terrible distraction."

I stepped forward. "I'm sorry. I was worried about you—"

"I have too much to do. Go back inside."

"What's wrong?"

"I should never have brought you here."

"Danton, stop!"

"There's no time. If I don't do this who will? No one else cares about the butterflies like I do."

"I care."

"I've been selfish. Ridiculous bringing you here so you can watch me fall apart." He faced me. "What kind of man does that to a woman he loves?"

"I want to be here."

"I'm selfish to the core." He yanked off his gloves and threw them down.

Moving quickly, I got close to him and cupped his face with my hands. "You're my everything. I'm under no illusion about what challenges are ahead for us, but we agreed we'd face this together."

He pushed me away. "I don't want you here."

"You don't mean that."

"Can't you see I'm busy? You're preventing me from getting my life in order."

Stepping back, I felt the ache in my chest burrow deeper.

"I have a car coming for you. I've left an envelope on the kitchen table with more than enough francs to take care of you. Go pack. Cameron will meet you at the airport."

"Don't."

"Now, please."

"Can we at least talk about it?"

"There's nothing else to discuss."

"What's changed?" I asked softly.

He looked distracted. "What?"

"Talk to me."

He shook his head. "I'm not ready."

"You have a new symptom?"

He raised his hands and stared at them.

"Your hands?"

"They're numb. It doesn't make any sense."

"Come here." I wrapped my arms around him and hugged him tight. "Cancel the car."

"You were never meant to be my nurse, Scarlet. I don't want this for you. Please, help me by going quietly. No fuss. I don't have the strength to fight you."

I broke away and walked over to the greenhouse. "I need some gloves."

"Remember me for who I am now. I don't want you to see me crumble."

"Okay, I'll use your gloves." I slipped them on and reached up and slid out a panel, giving it a tug, pulling it out of its frame.

A swarm of butterflies flew at my face. I squealed and tripped backward, tumbling onto the grass. I lay there watching them flutter above my body.

Danton loomed over me.

"Fuck everyone!" I snapped.

He lowered himself to the ground and stretched out beside me. "You can't be angry too."

"I can."

"You must never let negativity affect your mood."

"Are you serious?"

The multicolored insects swarmed above us.

I pointed. "It's a kaleidoscope of butterflies."

"Yes, it is."

I turned my head to look at him. "Now how else would I have

known that's what one calls a group of butterflies? You taught me that."

He reached up and let a butterfly land on his fingertip. We stared at it for the longest time.

"I'm staying," I whispered.

He took my hand and kissed my wrist.

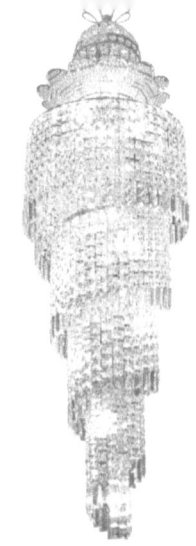

CHAPTER 19

France

A WOMAN'S VOICE CALLED OUT FROM THE FOYER AND I ROSE from my corner chair in the bedroom. Danton was fast asleep. I didn't want to wake him. He'd been sleeping a lot lately and I knew he needed it.

I left the bedroom and headed down the hallway, peering over the banister. My hands gripped the handrail when I saw a young dark-haired woman with two men standing behind her, both dressed in nursing scrubs. One of them pushed a wheelchair.

My friendly wave hid my dread as I made my way down.

The attractive woman began speaking to me in French.

I rested my hand on my heart in a gesture of sincerity. "My French isn't that good. I'm sorry—"

"American?"

"Yes."

"Where's my brother?"

"Danton? He's asleep." I glanced warily at the two men. "Why are you here?"

She pushed past me and headed up the stairs. "Are you his nurse?"

"Girlfriend."

She paused halfway up and stared back at me. The look on her face sent chills up my spine. "We're moving him to the hospital."

"But he wants to stay here."

"Don't put ideas in his mind." She continued climbing the stairs. "He needs to be surrounded by good people."

My world began to unravel as I followed her up the steps. I doubted I'd be able to make her respect Danton's wishes. I'd never even considered the possibility I would have to do battle with his family to fulfill his dying request. In all the months we'd been here, no one had ever visited us.

"Can we talk before you go in?" I hurried toward her. "Please don't wake him."

She burst into the bedroom.

I was panic-stricken when I realized there was no reasoning with her. She stood a few feet from the bed staring down at him and I saw no affection in her eyes, just a woman on a mission to get her own way.

"I'm Scarlet." I reached out and gently touched her on the arm. "I've been taking good care of him."

She jerked away. "How do you know him?"

"We're together."

I wanted to say we were lovers, but was unsure how much Danton wanted her to know about us.

Slowly, she turned to look at me. "You know who he is?"

"How do you mean?"

She narrowed her gaze to make her point. "You know he's one of the world's most famous cellists. Right?"

"He plays for me…" The words sounded so infantile when held up to the light of her revelation. My gaze fell on Danton as I tried to understand why he'd never shared that truth with me. He was always so humble and gracious.

And he'd wasted his talent on me.

He had given so much and yet so much was being asked of him now. His wish to die at home was going to be violated.

"He's so very good," I added softly.

"He's a profound maestro." She sighed. "Well, he was."

"He's not leaving here. This is what he wants."

She looked me up and down. "Like you have any say."

"Tilley?" Danton stirred and peered through one eye. "What are you doing here?"

She sat beside him on the edge of his bed. "I've been so worried about you, Danton. You didn't return my calls."

He pushed himself up. "Scarlet, can you close the curtains, please?"

I ran over to the window and pulled them shut.

"Why are you here?" He looked past her at the men. "Who are they?"

"They're with me."

"We agreed there would be no fuss."

She threw me a sharp glance. "You need to be in a place where people know how to care for you."

"Please tell them to leave."

The two men moved closer to the bed.

"Would you like to get some fresh air?" asked Tilley.

My gut wrenched at her deceit.

"Then will you give me some peace?" Weakly, Danton swung his legs over the bed and waved off any help. "I can manage."

In a flurry of activity, Danton was pulled out of bed and placed in the wheelchair.

"Danton?" I said in a panic, realizing he didn't understand what was happening.

Tilley glared at me. "Give us some privacy."

"It's okay, Scarlet" said Danton, trying to reassure me. "She's my sister. Go make us something to eat. We have that salmon. There's more than enough."

With Tilley leading the way, he was wheeled out of the room and down the corridor.

I followed them out. "This is not what he wants. Please, listen to him."

When they reached the top of the stairs, Danton was lifted out of the wheelchair and carried the rest of the way down.

"Danton, they're taking you away from here."

"We're just getting some fresh air." He reached back for me but I was too far away. "Walk with us. Tilley, you should see the garden. Scarlet's helped me keep it up."

At the bottom of the staircase, they placed him back into the wheelchair and he was pushed through the foyer.

And out through the front door.

Trembling, I grabbed at Tilley's arm.

She stopped suddenly and stared at me. "I'm having his will voided. He's not of sound mind."

"What will?" I asked.

She yanked her arm away. "Shame on you."

"No, I don't want anything. Please, don't take him away."

She slid open the back door of a large black minibus. "Say goodbye."

"What are you doing?" Danton looked panicked.

I sprinted toward the minibus and stood between Danton and the men.

"This is not negotiable," said Tilley. "You're too weak to stay here, Danton."

"Will you be with me?" He looked up at her. "Will you stay in the hospital when the time comes?"

She smiled at him. "It will be easier to visit you in Paris."

"Take me back in." Danton grabbed one of the men's arms.

"Hurry, please," Tilley said to the men. "We need to avoid rush hour." She glared at me. "Get your things. I'm locking up the house."

I threw my arms around Danton in a panic. "Tell them, Danton. Tell them what you want."

"Scarlet," he whispered.

"I'm not letting go."

He kissed my cheek. "The cavalry's here."

I followed his gaze toward the midday sun, shielding my eyes from the glare.

A long black Rolls Royce slid into the driveway and came to a stop before the house. Cameron Cole climbed out of the passenger side.

My heart leapt with relief.

I ran into his arms. "You have to help us."

"Cole. About fucking time." Danton waved at him. "Get me out of this thing."

"Who are you?" Tilley looked warily at Cameron.

"I'm his doctor," he said. "Gentlemen, take my patient back inside. Right away, please."

Allowing myself to breathe for the first time since Tilley had arrived, I watched Cameron follow Danton as he was wheeled back into the house.

I stood just outside the front door, my hands still trembling from the shock of almost losing Danton—and from the overwhelming relief I felt that Cameron had come to our rescue.

"Come on, Scarlet." Cameron tucked his hands into his pockets and glanced back at me. "That was one long flight. I need a cup of tea." He winked.

CHAPTER 20

France

WITH DANTON COMFORTABLE BACK IN HIS BED AND the house quiet again, I made myself busy in the kitchen.

Just as Danton had taught me, I prepared lunch for all three of us, placing three fresh salmon filets on a baking tray and sprinkling them with a little salt.

Cameron sat on a barstool at the center island, sipping his tea. "Thank you for all you've done for Danton."

"Of course." I lowered my gaze. "I only hope Tilley doesn't come back after she realizes you're still a medical student."

He shrugged. "I know as much as I need to…for this."

I shoved the baking tray into the oven and lifted the door shut. "You tricked me into going to Hillenbrand."

"I see you standing in a beautiful seaside house. Living with the man you love. The title 'Domestic Goddess' comes to mind."

I washed my hands under the faucet and wiped them with a tea towel. "You knew he was seriously ill?"

"Yes."

"And you knew I was suicidal?"

He held my gaze and gave a nod. I was more than a little annoyed with Cameron.

"How can you be sure that after he dies I won't be so grief-stricken that I end up killing myself?"

He looked away. "That would be a dreadful betrayal of Danton's wishes."

"I'm so…" I shook my head, unable to express how deeply I felt for him.

"Me too." He added a teaspoon of sugar to his tea. "What are his symptoms?"

"His hands go numb."

"His sight?"

"He's having difficulty seeing through his left eye. I told Doctor Pier. Nothing can be done, apparently."

"Thank you for taking such wonderful care of him."

"This is what he wants…to be here instead of in a hospital."

"And who wouldn't want that? To be surrounded by the ones you love."

My chest heaved. "Why does he have to die?"

Cameron came around and hugged me, a flash of vulnerability reflected in his gaze.

"How'd you meet him?" I asked.

Cameron sat back down on the barstool. "We were at boarding school together. He was a few years older than me."

"He never told me that."

He shrugged. "Even then he showed remarkable talent."

"Did he play for you, too?"

He nodded. "Like you, I was one of the lucky ones."

"When did you discover you had the same penchant for kink?"

"I spent a summer with him in Paris. He took me to a party. I was seventeen, but looked a little older because I'm so tall. He snuck me into a private club near the Boulevard de Clichy and I was mesmerized by the scene."

"BDSM?"

"Every kink imaginable." He gave me a lazy smile. "I was enthralled."

"That's why you opened D'envoûtement?"

"Yes. I realized there were others out there like us that needed a safe haven."

"And Danton spent time at Hillenbrand."

Cameron took a sip of tea.

"You knew he'd want me for himself when he saw me?"

"As I wanted you when you fell through my club's window."

"But you and I have never been lovers."

"Nor will we ever be. We must carve out a friendship that tolerates no intimacy of that nature."

"Because I will always belong to Danton?"

"You will."

Cello music carried through the house and I recognized it as Bach's *Prelude*. And it made me smile to think he was playing it again, the numbness leaving his hands as it sometimes did.

"His sister told me he's a famous musician."

"Yes, and there's quite a bit of speculation as to where he is right now."

"His sister's a little scary."

"Well, there's the will you see. There's a lot riding on it for her. His musical rights have to go to someone."

"Maybe a charity?"

He gave me a gentle smile. "I've taken some time off from Harvard. I'm here for the duration."

"Oh, Cameron. Thank you so much." I broke his gaze, not wanting to share how scared I'd been about facing the end with Danton alone. "The ocean's just a short walk away."

"I know."

"You've been here before?"

"Many times."

I studied him carefully. "Were you and Danton ever...lovers?"

Cameron placed his cup back onto its saucer.

A loud crash reverberated upstairs and the music came to an abrupt stop.

We ran from the kitchen, sprinted up the stairs, and flew into Danton's bedroom. To my horror, we found him lying on the floor, his cello beside him.

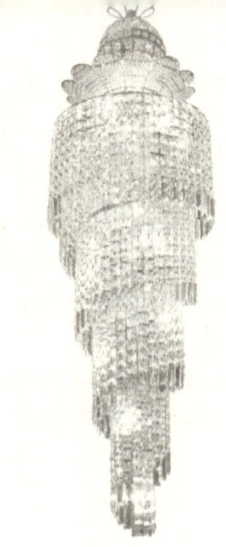

CHAPTER 21

France

DANTON LIKED FOR US TO READ TO HIM.
He sat up in bed with his back resting against the headboard and put in his requests for which books he wanted. Cameron and I would happily head off to the library to find novels by Charles Dickens or anything by Hemingway. Danton even made me read works from Edgar Allen Poe, and then he'd laugh when I acted freaked out over the macabre stories.

We spent the long days just talking and laughing at silly things, and I'd sit riveted as Danton and Cameron would reminisce about their time together at boarding school, or Cameron's time at Harvard, or Danton's recollections of studying music in Paris.

I'd massage Danton's hands to relax him. We were all comfortable enough to not be threatened by those long silences that brought the peace Danton needed for his headaches.

My education continued as they both chose subjects they thought I'd benefit from, like the arts or music or travel. They shared places they thought I should visit, many of them countries they'd both been to in the past.

As the days passed us by, I came to realize their closeness.

Our closeness.

We all appreciated the sacredness of our friendship and it felt as though we were becoming more…becoming a family.

The one I'd never had.

This was more than I'd envisioned true love to be, and though fearing his death, it also brought with it a stark reflection of the profoundness of life. Every butterfly that visited us through the open doors on those warm, lazy days and every bird's song that reached our ears became something sacred.

Danton's wishes would be honored and this house would remain a serene sanctuary—nothing but adoration would fill these rooms.

Together, Cameron and I turned Danton's bedroom into a beautiful space where nature and art morphed into one. I placed potted plants out on the balcony; daisies and bright colored roses, their soothing scent filling the room.

Cameron proved just how versatile he was when he worked high on a ladder in the center of Danton's bedroom, changing out the ordinary light fixture and hanging one of those upside-down tulips in its place.

More medical supplies were dropped off by Doctor Pier and Cameron reassured him he had everything covered and was more than qualified to provide the best care.

When Danton could no longer drink and the homemade soup I'd cooked for him could no longer be tolerated, Cameron set up an intravenous infusion in Danton's left arm to keep him hydrated and make him comfortable. Now and again he administered morphine to ease Danton's pain.

He slipped in and out of sleep.

The ocean glistened as the sun reflected off it by day and the moon by night.

We kept open the double doors of the balcony so he could enjoy the greenery, watch the birds swoop by and take in the sea view beyond, though his sight was fading now.

Despite everything, there was a sense of serenity.

There were no disagreements as there was nothing to argue about, merely a mutual respect that we were all here for each other.

That final evening started out like any other, with Cameron sitting on the bed on Danton's left and me snuggled up on his right, resting my head on my lover's chest and savoring his every heartbeat—breathing through the terror I felt but wanting to be strong for him.

Danton pressed his lips to my head in a warm kiss.

I raised my face to better see him, my brow furrowed in a question.

"Do you see how wonderful life is?" he asked weakly. "How important you are as part of it?"

I frowned, too saddened to speak.

"Scarlet, you've given me more than I knew possible," he said hoarsely. "You're so beautiful inside. Don't let the world take that away." He took a shallow breath. "Forgive those who do you harm. Don't let their betrayal poison you. Purge it and replace it with love. Embrace each moment. Look at what you've given me. You've given yourself completely." He closed his eyes. "What else is there?"

No. It was Danton who had given me strength and the ability to see that life could be glorious.

My death wish had long ago dissipated because of him, because he'd taught me to know myself and live authentically.

Cameron placed an EP on the corner record player and the beautiful sound of a cello filled the room. I knew it was one of Danton's recordings, a rendition by Bach.

Cameron sat back down and reached for Danton's hand.

I kissed Danton's cheek and pulled the blanket up and over him when he felt the cold. I stroked his hand to comfort me as much as him.

"Promise me something." Danton turned his head and looked at Cameron. "Protect her with your life...if it ever comes to it."

Cameron gave a nod of reassurance. "I promise."

I rested my head on Danton's chest once more, clinging to him as though that alone would keep him with me forever.

A Monarch butterfly fluttered in through the bedroom window and settled on the end of the bed.

"Funny, isn't it?" whispered Danton. "How butterflies get all the praise but it's the caterpillar that's struggled so very much to change."

"We know their struggle," said Cameron softly. "There's that at least."

"I love you Danton, so much." I forced back tears. "I always will."

He turned to me. "I'll always be here for you, Scarlet. I promise I'll come to you if you call for me." His fingers trailed through my hair. "If ever you need me just say my name."

The butterfly rose up and fluttered out of the window. I watched it until it flew out of sight.

CHAPTER 22

A Year Ago
Ethan's Home—Sherman Oaks

"DANTON," I SOBBED. "I'M AFRAID."

His presence was stronger than I'd ever experienced it before. Resting my head on Ethan's chest, I surrendered to the sense of peace that now came over me.

Ethan's hand caressed my scalp. "Hey, there."

I raised my head to look at him. "Thank God."

I'd been trying to wake him for what seemed like hours, but in reality it had been minutes.

"Where am I?" Ethan sat up.

"Your office."

Another kick at the door made him freeze.

"The phone's dead," I told him. "Who the hell is that?"

"It's okay. He's after me, not you." He used the desk to pull himself up and then staggered over to the safe.

Glaring at him, I pushed myself to my feet and stood. "You have a gun?"

"Yes." He lifted a print off the wall. "Are you hurt?"

"No."

"Sorry, Scarlet." He threw the picture down and set to work on opening the safe. "The police are on their way," he called out loudly, as though that might persuade the attacker to leave.

"My phone's in the car," I whispered.

He paused to wipe his brow, and cringed when he saw a smudge of blood. "What's wrong with my head?"

"It's a cut. Doesn't look deep," I reassured him. "A fan fell on you and you got knocked forward into the wall."

"Fuck."

I glanced around the room again as though some weapon might magically appear.

"How did we get in here?" he asked.

"I dragged you."

He mulled that over. "You saved my life?"

"I suppose."

Ethan blinked, shaking his head. "Shit."

His nimble fingers went back to working the safe's rotary mechanism, clicking it around, his expression fraught with concentration. He yanked the door open and reached inside.

"You might want to keep it somewhere a little more handy next time," I said.

"I was hoping all this was over." He pulled out a handgun and gestured to the right side of the door. "Come on."

We hurried over and shoved our backs against the wall. He removed the safety and raised the gun.

"Do you think he's gone?" I whispered.

"Doubt it."

"You know who it is?"

"Drug cartel."

"The people who shot your wife?"

He gave a nod. "Sorry you got dragged into this."

"Did you know they'd come back?"

"Thought it was a possibility."

I looked at him aghast. "Do you think there's more than one?"

"Hit men work alone."

"Oh, no, Cameron's on his way."

An expression of grim determination flashed across Ethan's face. I grabbed his sleeve. "It's too dangerous."

"Stay here." He unlocked the door quietly and slid out.

If I could get to my car I'd be able to call the police. Better still, Ethan had dropped his phone in the living room and if I could just get to it...

This was the worst day of my life.

No, the worst day was when I'd lost Danton.

Had he just been with me? Had that sense of peace I'd felt really been him comforting me? Even if it hadn't been him, I knew Danton would want me to fight back.

I made a run for it, heading back down the hallway in the direction I'd come. There, near the bar on the floor, lay Ethan's Smartphone. I knelt down and reached for it.

A pair of dirty running shoes suddenly appeared in front of me.

Raising my gaze, I looked into the barrel of a gun. The Latino man lifted me up and turned me around, hugging my back into his chest. The barrel of his gun met my temple and pressed into it painfully.

Terror gripped my throat like a vice. I could barely breathe.

Cameron's face came into view, and my heart began pounding even more furiously when I realized the danger he was in.

"I'm unarmed." Cameron raised his hands to prove it and threw me a reassuring smile.

God, this man was confronting a cold-blooded killer and acting like he was in control.

"Stay there," the Latino man yelled.

Cameron's expression remained calm. "I will. Tell me what you need. I'm a doctor."

The man's grip tightened around my throat, and I gasped.

"Ethan Neilson ran off." Cameron held his hands higher. "We won't tell anyone we saw you. Please let her go. She has nothing to do with any of this."

The hit man jabbed his gun harder against my temple. "Come any closer."

"Not that it's any of my business," said Cameron. "But that mole on your wrist...might wanna get it checked out. Again, none of my business. Not sure why I brought it up. I'm an idiot, apparently. Need to work on my boundaries. This shit's making me nervous."

The pressure left my temple as the man glanced at his wrist.

A gunshot rang out, and the stranger released his grip.

I heard a heavy thump behind me, and turned to see my attacker lying on the floor...dead.

I bolted toward Cameron and he opened his arms.

"Scarlet." He hugged me tight. "Jesus Christ."

I followed his gaze and saw Ethan still pointing his gun at the man.

Cameron let me go and went over to our attacker, kicking the gun away from his hand. He knelt close to him and placed two fingers on his carotid. Then he gave Ethan a nod of reassurance.

Ethan staggered backward against the wall and slid down it.

"Where's your first aid kit?" asked Cameron.

"Kitchen," said Ethan, staring dead ahead at nothing. "Last cupboard on the left."

"I'll get it." I went to search for it, my hands still shaking.

When I came back, they both looked like they were in the middle of a standoff.

"What's going on?" I broke open the first aid kit.

Cameron slipped on a pair of non-latex gloves, ripped open a package of gauze and dabbed Ethan's forehead laceration.

"It was self defense," he told Ethan. "You have witnesses. Scarlet, call 911."

Ethan pushed himself up. "He shot my wife."

Cameron gestured toward my phone. "Scarlet, make the call."

"Ethan, you were unconscious," I said. "We need to call an ambulance."

"Wait," snapped Ethan as he glanced over at the dead man. "That's Leon Quintono, of the Quintono Cartel."

Cameron paused for a second and stared up at me as though the name should mean something.

"It's not like I can prosecute him," added Ethan.

I lowered my phone. "What are you saying?"

"If the cartel find out I killed one of their own, they'll send someone else for me. Look, I just need a minute to think this through." He shoved Cameron's hand away.

"What about police protection?" I said.

"Shit," whispered Cameron. "Once it comes out we were here and we're witnesses to a cartel hit…"

I tried to swallow the lump in my throat. "Would the cartel come after us, too?"

Ethan glanced up at me. "That's a certainty."

"What are we going to do?" I asked.

Ethan shrugged. "We're all fucked, apparently. Welcome to my club. Not quite as fun as *your* club, obviously. But as you can see it gets the blood pumping."

"As a psychiatrist," said Cameron, "I'm diagnosing you with Asshole Syndrome."

"Wouldn't be the first time."

Ethan grabbed the gauze out of Cameron's hand and dabbed his forehead, flinching at the pain it caused. "Where was that music coming from?"

"I didn't hear anything," I said, tucking my phone into my pocket.

"Back in the office." Ethan looked up at me. "You sure you didn't hear it? I woke up and heard it playing."

All I'd heard was a dead silence, and my own ragged breathing.

Ethan pressed his fingers to his temple. "It sounded like a cello."

Slowly, Cameron turned his head and stared up at me.

CHAPTER 23

I JOINED ETHAN AND CAMERON IN THE GARDEN.

They were sitting on a wooden bench, deep in conversation. Ethan was holding a packet of cigarettes and Cameron was berating him playfully for wanting to smoke one. For some reason, after all we'd been through, that made me smile.

The same care had been taken out here to create a soothing landscape, with a lush green lawn and gorgeous palm trees. There was a long hedge with flowerbeds running along the front of it that gave off the most wonderful scent. I wondered if his wife had planted them. Ethan didn't strike me as the gardening type.

On any other day it would have been heavenly to sit out here.

All I could think of was Ethan's comment about hearing a cello. There was no other explanation for it other than Danton's presence had been with me.

"My sweet, sweet Danton," I whispered.

Staring up at the starlit sky I sent out a silent prayer to him and hugged myself, allowing the memory of him to comfort me and a stillness to envelop me, despite everything.

Cameron saw me across the garden. "Hey, you okay?"

I headed in their direction.

"Scarlet, you saved my life." Ethan gave me a grateful smile. "Thank you."

"Of course."

Ethan lit up a cigarette and took a long drag. "I just shot a man dead."

Cameron glanced at me. "It was self-defense. No one will argue against that. I'm trying to persuade him to go to Cedars."

"Ethan," I said, "you were out cold. You could have a concussion. You need a CT scan."

"I'm fine," he said.

Cameron shook his head. "No, you're not."

"Shay's on his way." I'd just called him.

"Who's Shay?" Ethan blew out smoke and it spiraled.

"My head of security." Cameron gave a shrug. "He's ex-special forces and will know what to do if you really want to proceed with this madness. I'm concerned your head injury is clouding your judgment, Ethan."

I knelt before Ethan and rested my hand on his knee. "This is not what we do. We don't go around hiding bodies."

Cameron agreed with a nod. "We're losing time. The coroner will know we delayed calling them. Livor mortis is setting in—"

"I'd rather face off with the cartel than break the law," I said.

"Really?" snapped Ethan. "You do realize Leon played with us first? They'll skin us alive and then hang our corpses in the street."

"First of all," said Cameron, "you're intention was to prosecute us. Remember that little detail? This case just got a whole lot more complicated for you."

"And kind of convenient for you." Ethan glared at him.

"That's right," snapped Cameron. "I paid a visit to the Quintono Cartel earlier today. Popped in there for a Mexican beer and your name came up."

"I didn't mean that."

"How exactly did Leon get away with killing your wife?" I asked. "How did he walk free?"

"Legal technicality," said Ethan. "Or, as we like to put it, they got to the jurors."

I cringed. "What happened?"

"They killed one of them." Ethan leaned forward. "I'm gonna throw up."

"That's it," said Cameron. "I'm either calling an ambulance or you'll let me take you to the hospital. I'll speed you through admissions."

"You work there?" Ethan rose to his feet.

"Yes." Cameron jumped up and grabbed his arm to steady him.

Ethan arched a curious brow. "Where do you get the time? What with a club and a private practice?"

"I make time."

We headed through the garden toward the house.

Cameron glanced back at me. "Go home."

"No, I'm coming with you," I said. "Maybe we can say we weren't here when Leon got shot? Maybe we don't need to be mentioned at all?"

Cameron opened the door. "Let's see what Shay comes up with."

"I've never broken the law in my life," said Ethan.

"Not even a parking ticket?" Cameron asked, as he entered the house ahead of us.

I slammed into his back when he stopped suddenly. There was the shadow of a man leaning over Leon's body.

It was Shay.

His Nike pants and shoes proved we'd interrupted his evening run and his hair was still ruffled from working out.

Shay's loyalty went back years and Chrysalis couldn't have prevailed so smoothly without him. This man was an expert when it came to protecting our interests as well as those of our clients.

Seeing him here made me sigh with relief.

"So I take it this is our man?" Shay glanced at the corpse.

Cameron rolled his eyes. "I was tempted to write 'I'm the dead one' on his forehead for you."

Shay smirked and held out his hand to shake Ethan's. "Shay Gardner." He looked over at me. "You guys okay?"

"Not really," I said.

Shay gave a nod of understanding. "Firstly, I'm glad you called me. Secondly, Scarlet, what the fuck?"

"It was a good thing I was here," I said. "Can we discuss this later? I'm worried about Ethan. He might have a concussion."

"But…no police?" said Shay. "Seriously?"

"We need your advice." Cameron patted Ethan's back. "The dead man tried to kill them. He's a member of a cartel. Or should I say 'was.'"

"Are you fucking kidding me?" said Shay. "Please tell me you're not asking me to get rid of the body?"

"Technically, yes," said Cameron.

"In front of a D.A?"

"I'm the one asking," said Ethan.

Shay glared at us.

"We're open to suggestions." Cameron gestured to the body.

"This is not what I do," said Shay.

"I respect that." Cameron swapped a wary glance with me. "I know I'm asking a lot."

A ringtone of Beethoven's *Für Elise* sang out.

"Don't answer it," snapped Shay. "The call will be recorded as this being your location at his time of death."

Ethan walked over and picked his cell up from the floor. "I have to. It's Judge Reynolds." He leaned on the bar to steady himself and took the call.

"Fucking fantastic," whispered Shay.

Cameron gestured for him to be quiet. "Can you help us or not?"

Shay was seething. "Let me think."

Ethan closed his eyes. "Do you want me to fly out there? I can get the next flight to Vegas."

We all stood staring at him, not wanting to believe this latest bit of madness.

Ethan continued speaking, his voice surprisingly calm, "I'm so sorry, Alison. I'm here for you. Call me if you need anything." He ended the call and turned to face us.

"What's going on?" asked Shay.

Ethan had gone pale. "That wasn't the judge, it was his wife. He was shot dead over an hour ago. Looks like Leon got to him first."

"They're taking everyone out," Cameron said.

"I'm calling the coroner." Shay raised his phone.

Cameron closed his eyes for a second. "Baxter?"

"Who's Baxter?" Ethan asked. "A member of Chrysalis?"

"Let's go get you a CT scan," said Cameron. "I, for one, am eager to see if there's anything in your skull."

"That's unfair," said Ethan.

"Really? You refused police protection, didn't you?" Cameron guided him out the front door. "Someone has a death wish."

Cameron glanced back at me.

CHAPTER 24

"THANK YOU FOR THIS." ETHAN STOOD AT MY FRONT DOOR looking bedraggled.

His usual arrogant demeanor was gone and I marveled at how humbled he looked.

We'd almost lost our lives this afternoon. I'd refused to cry, refused to give that bastard who'd almost shot me at point blank range any power over me.

But I was still shaken and I could see Ethan was, too.

Staring behind him into the dusky night I saw Cameron's BMW driving off. My gaze drifted back to Ethan and the bandage on his forehead. His white shirt was crinkled and his pants were creased. He was also missing his belt—probably removed when he'd had his CT scan. He was holding an overnight bag.

I gave him a polite smile. "Come in."

He stepped inside. "The CT scan turned out fine."

"Thank goodness."

"They wanted to keep me overnight. I signed out AMA." He sighed. "I promised Cameron I'd come here and have you observe me for any signs of imminent death, as if I'd be so lucky. Thank you for inviting me over."

"I'm glad you're here. Talking about today will be good for both of us."

He studied my face and cringed. "You didn't know I was coming?"

"It's fine."

"Yeah…this isn't awkward."

"I want you here."

"I can Uber home."

"You don't want to go home, surely?"

He gave a shrug.

"Stay. I need company right now."

"If you're sure."

I led him into the sitting room.

He stared at the elegant cello resting on a stand in the corner and his gaze met mine.

"You play?"

"It belonged to a dear friend. He wanted me to have it."

"I heard a cello playing, remember?"

I shrugged. "I'm as baffled as you."

"That was kind of weird," Ethan said.

I wanted to believe it, needed to, but was still feeling too fragile to entertain the idea that Danton had come back to me.

"I've often felt guilty for keeping his cello. I should give it to a talented musician, but I just can't part with it."

"It's gorgeous."

"Danton would play for me." There was that familiar pang of loss. "I found out after he'd died he was one of France's prominent musicians. He played at Carnegie Hall. I was naive back then and had no idea how truly talented he was. I loved it when he played, but it wasn't until afterward that I really knew of his greatness. Those final months with him were profound."

"You were lovers?"

"Yes."

"I'm so sorry. How did he die?"

"He had a brain tumor."

He looked devastated for me.

I forced a grin. "We both understand what it is to lose someone special."

He gave a nod and cleared his throat. "I play the sax," he said, changing the subject, clearly uncomfortable with the intimacy.

"I remember Cameron mentioning it."

A coy expression crossed his face, as though he, too, remembered that awkward exchange in Cameron's office. Ethan looked so much more fragile than I'd ever seen him and Cameron knew I wouldn't turn him away. Not after everything we'd both been through.

Ethan set his bag on the floor. "I wasn't sure where else to go. I'm not the most popular person, as you've no doubt discovered."

I suppressed a smile.

"You know how it goes. I'm the alcohol police if you're driving home. No smoking pot in front of me." He scratched his neck. "Pay my taxes on time. Never late on a bill. No porn."

"You're squeaky clean then?"

"Squeaky has nothing on me."

"Well, you're welcome here if you don't mind hanging out with a fallen woman."

"A fallen woman who saved my life." After a thoughtful pause, he said, "Cameron was kind enough to find some new clothes for me."

"He's good like that."

Ethan walked over and pulled me into a hug.

Closing my eyes, I savored the physical contact, his warmth soothing me, and I rose onto my toes and kissed his cheek. "Stay here for as long as you like."

"How can you be so kind after how I treated you?"

"That's who we are, Ethan," I said, stepping back to look up at him. "You can't shock us. You can't make us hate you because we know too much about the human condition. "

"You're more forgiving than me."

"I believe that's the point. I heard somewhere that 'love is the art of continuous forgiveness.'"

"Going home is gonna be hard." His lips trembled. "All my memories of her are there."

"I understand."

"That fucker desecrated those memories."

"Come and sit down." I gestured toward the couch.

Ethan noticed the ocean view. "Wow."

"Yes, it's quite something."

"You live alone?"

"Yes."

"No man in your life?"

"And no woman." I gave him an amused look.

"Oh, you're bi?"

"Yes."

"But no one special right now?"

"No."

"Cameron? You two have never…?"

"He's like a brother to me. We made the decision a long time ago that sex was off limits."

Ethan raised an eyebrow, as if he found our arrangement hard to believe.

"Let's order in food. I didn't have time to shop. Being attacked by a drug cartel seems to take up all my time these days."

"That'll teach you to trespass," he said, winking at me.

And for a split second he reminded me of Danton, the way he'd stare at me like Ethan was doing now with pure kindness in his eyes.

I strolled into the kitchen. "I'll get the menu."

He followed me and I slid open the drawer and pulled out the restaurant brochure.

"Shay took care of our problem," he said.

"What problem?"

"Apparently, they don't want me to know where the body went. New hardwood floors were installed. The whole thing's fucked up."

"I have no idea what you're talking about."

"You guys really own my balls now. Don't you?"

"That's not how it works."

"That's how it always works."

"Not with us, Ethan. You see decadence when you look at us. Indulgence. What we really are to those who know us are people who believe in forgiveness. Kindness. Understanding. Fulfillment. We take love-making to an ethereal level."

"Yeah, well, sex is behind me now." He threw up his arms. "As you've discovered."

"You don't know that."

"Actually, I've tried everything to fix my…issue. Oh, this is not embarrassing at all."

"You can tell me anything. I'm good with secrets."

"You're surprisingly easy to talk to."

"So are you."

"I'm an arrogant bastard and we both know it," he said, grinning. "Do you have any beer?"

"Yes, of course."

"This place is very you. Chic. Eclectic. You have a French flair."

I laid the menu down on the counter and got to work on prying open two bottles of Miller Lite.

I handed him one. "I forgot to ask if you like Chinese food."

Ethan came closer. "Yes." He smiled. "I'm sure men tell you this all the time and it's the most inappropriate thing I'll ever say to you, I promise." He stared into my eyes. "You're the most beautiful woman I've ever met, Scarlet. I haven't looked at another woman since…"

"I'm sure she made you happy."

"She was a pediatric nurse."

I took a sip of beer. "We can talk about her if you like."

"Later, maybe."

After I placed our order, we settled in the living room and chatted for a while. When our food arrived, we went outside to the balcony to enjoy the sunset, settling in the rocking chairs and sipping beer. Ethan tucked into his orange chicken like he was starved, but I only picked at my cashew chicken. My appetite was still off.

Hours slipped away at a comfortable pace as I rocked in my chair, listening to Ethan share his life story. He talked about his time at Emory University in Georgia and his passion for law. He'd met his wife at a friend's wedding in San Francisco. He'd ended up in California to be closer to her family. Now, he was seriously contemplating returning to Georgia.

The silences between us felt natural.

When the sea breeze became too chilly we headed back in and talked some more. Eventually, Ethan fell asleep on my couch and I pulled one of my soft throws over him, careful not to wake him.

I headed to the bathroom, needing to find a way to relax and decided on a warm bath. I carried my second beer with me and set it down on the edge of the sink.

Watching the tub fill, I breathed in the relaxing scent of vanilla mixed with lavender that rose with the steam. I actually felt a sense of peace that Ethan was here. I was reassured he'd be safe—for a while, at least, as no one else would know he was here. Shay and Cameron would have made sure of that.

My thoughts drifted, and suddenly I had a terrible flashback of being held at gunpoint.

A chill shot up my spine.

Any sense of control I'd had was merely an illusion. How quickly our lives can be turned upside down. The pathway we are on so easily decimated, leaving everything unrecognizable.

I'd learned long ago what true love felt like and since that day I'd never again experienced it so profoundly. I'd been with other men, of course, but no single man had ever affected me as deeply as Danton had. I hadn't been so intrigued by another man until Ethan, and the fact that his fierce arrogance was used for the service of others had a sexy edge to it.

And that fricken southern accent made my clit throb.

Jesus, Scarlet, get a grip.

I pulled off my sweater and unzipped my jeans and removed them, placing them inside the hamper. I stripped out of my underwear and placed my bra and panties in there, too.

I was about to get in the tub when I heard Ethan call out from behind the door.

"Scarlet?"

"Yes."

A moment of quiet lingered.

"Are you okay?" I asked.

"Can I come in?"

"I'm taking a bath."

"I heard the water running."

"I didn't mean to wake you. There's another bathroom down the hall. To the left."

He went silent again.

We were such opposites and yet...

My mind carried me back to those moments of us in Chrysalis's dungeon, a mistress and sub whose chemistry was undeniable, an undercurrent of passion taut with its denial. That need to touch him was an extraordinary vortex that I yearned to be drawn into.

"I'm sorry, I shouldn't have bothered you," he said.

"Do you want to bathe with me?"

He twisted the door handle and stepped in, blinking as his gaze swept over my breasts and down to my sex. "Jesus, you're beautiful." He spun round and faced the door. "Sorry."

"Look at me."

He combed his fingers through his hair. "Not sure what I was thinking. Bit impulsive. It's been a long day."

I recalled how he'd reacted during our session, how in the quiet moments he'd pined to be touched by me, caressed and stroked to the point of pleasure.

"Would you like to fuck me?" I whispered it.

"We both know that's impossible." He started to leave.

"Wait." I stepped forward and touched his back to encourage him to turn around.

Slowly, he faced me.

I rested my palm against his face. "Try not to think so much."

Working on his shirt buttons first, I began to undress him and he relaxed a little as I unzipped his pants. He slid them off along with his underwear and socks, throwing everything in the corner.

His cock really was a thing of beauty, even as it hung between his thighs in a testament to his pain, unable to be aroused.

Ethan reached out and caressed my left breast, running a finger over the sensitized nipple. "God, you're stunning."

I let my gaze sweep over his nakedness in appreciation, showing him how gorgeous he was to me.

I gestured to the bath.

He climbed in and then reached out to take my hand, guiding me as I stepped in to join him. I stood in the welcome warmth and turned my back on him. Water swooshed around us as we sat down. I laid my back against his chest and my legs between his. He wrapped his arms around me.

"See how nice this is?" I reached for the sponge and caressed his calf.

"Can I touch you?"

"Yes."

"I mean *touch* you."

"I'm not going to come, Ethan." I turned to look at him.

"Even if I want you to?"

"No. It doesn't seem fair for me to come if you don't."

"It's payback, baby," he said with a Cary Grant accent. "You've been flaunting your beauty since I've met you."

Laughing, I relaxed and let my head rest against his chest, my thighs parting slightly.

He nuzzled into my hair. "You smell amazing."

He reached around my waist and his hands dipped lower, cupping me between my thighs. That first caress of his fingers sent pleasure coursing through me. He tenderly explored, easing apart my folds and flicking my clit with a brilliant precision, slowly at first and then faster, setting a perfect rhythm.

My inner wetness grew as his fingers continued their delicate strumming, his breaths heavy with desire.

He let out a long sigh. "I feel pleasure. Just can't get the fucking thing up."

Guilt washed over me that I was about to go where he couldn't, rise higher than he ever would, my thighs trembling, my back arching as I neared climax.

I nudged his hand away.

His left hand gripped my throat in a strike of power.

Just as Danton had once done.

I froze.

"Ethan?" His name slipped from me like a quiet plea.

His show of domination sent me reeling and had my clit throbbing for more. I pushed back letting him know I liked his flash of dominance.

"This is not about you, Scarlet." He let go of my throat and plunged his fingers between my thighs again, flicking.

I gripped the tub as bliss stole my ability to resist rising higher. "Ethan."

"Come for me."

Letting go, spine arching, I gave him what he demanded of me and came hard, writhing against him, my thoughts scattering as I climaxed, my sex clenching for him, my heart aching that I'd never feel him inside me.

This was the intimacy I'd craved when I'd first met him and it blew my mind we'd made it here, to this place of closeness and understanding. He had been my enemy, this man who had threatened to destroy my world, and yet now Ethan was fulfilling it in the most glorious way.

Drifting in and out of bliss, we stayed in the bath for a while, topping up the water as both heat and time evaporated, continuing to comfort each other.

He explored me further, sending me into a frenzy as he pumped two fingers inside me while his right hand flicked my clit, slowly at first, and then fast enough to cause my body to go rigid as another orgasm consumed me.

As I came again and again, I realized Ethan needed so very much to see he could still pleasure a woman...see he was still desirable.

I wanted to give him more of me and see him healed.

We let the water drain from the bath and stepped out, taking our time drying each other off. The continued intimacy was what we both needed, as though the cruelness of today could be endured no other way.

Not wanting to be apart, we headed off to bed together. I'd taken such pleasure in decorating my tranquil room with its refined Asian design. The leather headboard added the final touch of simple comfort, the lighting soft and inviting.

We lay facing each other with our heads resting on the two plush pillows, snuggled cozily beneath the satin duvet and holding hands like lovers who'd known each other for years—not like a couple who'd been going at each other in an argument just this morning.

"How are you doing?" he whispered.

"Good." I smiled at him.

"I like being with you."

"This is all very unexpected. One minute you're threatening to shut my club down and the next we're in bed."

"That's how I roll, baby."

He made me laugh.

My fingertip ran over a small scar on his chin.

"Fell off my bicycle as a kid. Wish I could say I got it doing something more impressive, like wrestling an alligator."

"I have one on my knee. Got it wrestling a croc." I gave him my best *oh yeah, got one up on you buddy* look.

"I can't believe you're not married," he said.

"I'm pretty choosy."

"I'm honored then. You've let me in."

"Not so long ago I thought you didn't like me."

He broke my gaze. "Sorry I treated you so harshly. In the dungeon you took my breath away and it scared me."

"Why?"

"Well, other than my impending threat to charge you and shut down Chrysalis, I could see myself becoming obsessed with you." He cringed. "I'm going to scare you off."

"You had me mesmerized, too, Ethan. It's that accent. Does things to me."

He waggled his eyebrows. "Careful, that's an invitation for me never to shut up."

I dragged my teeth over my lip suggestively.

"Can't believe I'm lucky enough to be with the sexiest woman alive." His eyes devoured me.

"You've not dated since your wife?"

"Women tend to want a man who can deliver the goods. When was the last time you dated seriously?"

"Danton."

"How long ago?"

"A long time."

"You've never gotten close to someone since him?"

"Yes, but there's never been anyone like him. He was pretty special."

"Tell me more."

"He was a beautiful man. Sweet and strong and brilliant."

"A lot to live up to then?"

"Yes."

"Do you think that's why you've never married?"

I nodded.

"How did you meet him?"

"Cameron introduced me, in a roundabout way."

"How do you mean?"

"Promise not to be shocked?"

"I'll try. But there's no telling with you."

I smirked. "I was a member of Cam's first club. He was concerned about me. I was reckless. I'd shown signs of suicidal tendencies."

He looked horrified. "Something happened to you?"

"My parents disowned me. I spent my childhood in foster care. Ran away from the last family I was with. They were a little cruel. Got a job working as a bartender in Massachusetts. I broke into Cameron's club and he took me under his wing. He used his influence to get me into Harvard. Before that he worked out a strategy that would help me see life was worth living. He placed me in Danton's care."

"How did Danton help you?"

"He showed me how to live." My lips trembled at the sacred memory of him and the words he'd told me. "How to...seize opportunities."

Ethan reached out and touched my cheek. "I don't think it's a coincidence that I heard a cello."

"Do you really think it was him?"

"I can't think of any other explanation."

I tilted my head. "You don't seem like the type of man who would believe in the mystical."

"You don't really know me."

"I want to," I replied, smiling. "After Danton passed away I found out he'd sent funds to a Swiss bank account in my name. Money to pay for university. He was concerned his will might be contested by his family. So he planned ahead. It's because of him I have a PhD."

"What a great guy."

"He saved my life. I'm forever indebted to him."

"He obviously loved you a great deal."

"During our time in the dungeon, you muttered something about your wife going in first?"

His eyebrows shot up in surprise. "I did?"

"Yes."

"I must have spaced out or something." He let out a sigh. "We'd come home from the supermarket, just around the corner. She went on ahead into the house. I was locking the car and bringing the rest of the bags in. Leon was already inside. He shot her in the head before she could deactivate the alarm. Then he ran. I always felt it should have been me that died. Still, we got the bastard in the end, didn't we?"

"I'm so sorry."

"That was four years ago now."

"Think about a session with Cameron, please."

"This is not how I saw my day going, lying in bed with the most beautiful woman in the world."

"Ethan, you could swear at me and it would sound sexy."

He laughed. "How the hell can a day start off so shitty and end up so incredible?"

"You have to accept police protection. Please. I'm scared for you."

He looked away.

"They're going to come back for you when they hear you're still alive."

"Funny isn't it."

"What?"

His intense blue eyes met mine. "I didn't have anything to live for until now."

CHAPTER 25

ETHAN PACED IN CAMERON'S OFFICE.

It was reminiscent of that time he'd been in here after our fake session, only now he was on our side.

He stopped and stared at him. "Cole, how does it work again?"

Cameron tucked his hands into his pockets and leaned back against his desk. "I will storm into your psyche and rip it apart until it gives us what we need. I will be your advocate, your knight in shining armor."

Ethan flinched. "That doesn't sound fucked up at all."

"I'll be waiting right here," I told him.

Ethan gave me a nod and turned to glare at Cameron again. "Can something go wrong?"

"I have a hundred percent success rate." Cameron straightened his back. "After your session I'll give Scarlet to you. She'll be your sub or domme. You choose. You're an alpha, I respect that, but you also have a desire to be dominated. That officially makes you a switch."

"Just when I think I can't feel more embarrassed," he said.

I resisted frowning at Cameron, even though his methods were meant to be brilliant. Still, there was always a first time for something to go wrong and I didn't want it to be with Ethan's case.

I'd fallen for him, there was no denying that. Fallen for his gorgeous face, that sexy southern drawl, and the way he blushed when on the verge of arousal.

Ethan looked over at me. "Tell me it will work."

"I believe it will. Dr. Cole's the best there is."

Cameron gave me a smile. "Has Penny prepared the dungeon?"

I nodded.

"Inform Mr. Booth we're ready."

They'd both cleared their schedules for the week and Ethan had taken time off work.

Ethan rubbed his jaw. "An entire week?"

"It's the only way. It must be intensive."

"How does it work? What happens in there?"

"We're locked in a room and none of us leaves until the job is done."

"Fucking hell."

"We most certainly hope so. Ready?"

Ethan gave a reluctant nod. A call was placed to the dungeon master and a pretty submissive was sent to Cameron's office.

Arianna arrived wearing only a choker. She knelt before Ethan and stared up at him lovingly.

He looked a little lost for a moment as he blinked down at her, obviously trying to wrap his head around the fact he was really doing this. His incredulous stare found mine.

I offered a comforting smile.

"See you on the other side," he said.

"I'll be waiting."

"I've lost my mind." He froze, like they always do, doubting, questioning himself, realizing that this was either a stroke of genius or complete madness. "Please let it work."

"Arianna," said Cameron. "Take our client to the nirvana room."

I moved over to Ethan and embraced him. "Thank you for trusting us."

"All part of my death wish, apparently." He gave a nod to Arianna to let her know he was ready.

"By the time I've finished with you," said Cameron, "You'll know bliss again."

"Wish I'd come here sooner then." Ethan winked at me. "Here goes everything."

With a gesture from Cameron, Arianna rose to her feet and took Ethan's hand, leading him out.

The door closed behind them.

Cameron turned to face me. "He's fallen hard for you."

"Is that what you see?"

"Is that what you want me to see?"

"Yes."

"Come here." He pulled me over to the full length mirror at the back of the room and positioned me in front of him, wrapping his arms around me. "You're extraordinary. Of course he's fallen head over heels for you."

My reflection stared back: an empowered mistress, a sensual woman, a sultry vixen who knew the art of a man's pleasure and the way to soothe his soul.

Yet, remarkably, Ethan was saving mine.

Cameron's reflection looked exquisite as shadows danced over his dashing face. And my thoughts lingered a while on those memories of us in France, how perfect it had been, just him and me and Danton during those final weeks.

Danton would always own a piece of my heart.

Always.

Cameron's hand rested on my belly. "There's a cure for him. And you're looking at her."

"Please don't hurt him."

"A little pain never hurt anyone." He arched a brow.

I elbowed his stomach. "Do you think he could ever love me?"

"He already does."

CHAPTER 26

I T WAS MY TURN TO PACE IN CAMERON'S OFFICE.

Something was wrong.

Dreadfully wrong.

I could feel it surging through my veins and chilling my blood, an internal alarm that never failed to warn me when danger threatened.

Ethan had been locked away in that dungeon for too long.

A week had come and gone and it had never taken Cameron this long to get a result. Yes, he had an impressive success rate, though due to patient confidentially he never discussed his methods. They'd been whispers, of course, of just how controversial they actually were. His unusual technique of locking up a client in a dungeon until he acquired the desired result wasn't exactly mentioned in the *Journal of Psychiatry*.

Cameron had used a similar method on me, but instead of him performing the therapy himself he'd entrusted me to Danton.

Inside that beautiful greenhouse, that cool breeze brushing over my nakedness, those beautiful butterflies flittering around me, my secret spilling within the safety of that glass cocoon as Danton reached a place inside me no one ever had.

Right now, Ethan was meant to be wrapped in a nurturing environment just as profound, but could Cameron succeed where everyone else had failed? We knew his methods usually worked, we'd seen the evidence time and time again as his patients withdrew from that dungeon reborn, as profoundly as a butterfly flying free from a chrysalis—a metamorphosis like no other.

I'd tried to keep busy.

Really, I had.

I'd managed Cole's office and taken his calls and dealt with all the humdrum details that went along with having Chrysalis run smoothly. I had my own clients, too, that needed nurturing back at Enthrall. Lotte and Penny, my fellow dominatrixes, knew all too well my will to not disrupt the session was failing and had even strongly advised me to leave Chrysalis until it was over.

But I'd promised Ethan I would stay close in case he needed me. *Insanity.*

My addled brain was suggesting mutiny…that in some other universe it was okay to break into a room mid-session and rescue the client from Cameron's therapeutic clutches.

Was he pushing Ethan too far?

Cameron hated failure and no doubt he'd been pushing Ethan way more than was ethical. I couldn't stand by and let him take this beautiful man through one more minute of torturous therapy.

I mean, all those other experts had failed, hadn't they? Were we arrogant to believe we could achieve what those brilliant minds hadn't? Ethan was going to have to find a new way to face this.

No, don't do it.

My conscience warned me to turn back and yet my feet continued to hurry through the foyer and down the steps toward the dungeons, my chest tightening as I neared the door, hands shaking, my imagination running wild with what I would face. A broken man lying on the floor? Cameron's wrath for interrupting them? Richard's amusement that I'd tipped my hand, proving I'd fallen for Ethan?

With a shove I pushed open the door.

A waft of cologne, leather, and the heady scent of power.

Stillness.

A central chain held up a leather harness in the center. I knew Ethan had been strapped into it at some point. Candles burned to the wick. Soft lighting that my eyes grew accustomed to. A pizza box in the corner. One of Richard's sweaters thrown over the back of a chair.

With my throat tight, I backed out and bumped straight into a body. Turning sharply, I saw a scantily clad Arianna, her choker secure around her throat, her dark hair curling down and around her shoulders, nipples pert from the cold.

A pang of jealousy hit me that she'd spent time with him.

"Where are they?" I asked.

"They left."

"I can see that. What happened?"

She gave a shrug. "It's over. Obviously."

Raising my chin high I assumed dominance. "Where are they?"

She measured her words carefully. "At Cameron's."

"Beverly Hills?"

"Yes."

"Why did they leave?"

"I don't know."

I softened my tone. "How did Ethan look?"

"Ask Dr. Cole. I'm not allowed to discuss it."

"Were you in there?"

She raised her hand defensively. "It was just Master Cole and Master Booth. I'm only here to make sure all personal items are out before they clean."

My gaze returned to the room and I tried to fathom why Cameron hadn't told me it was over. He knew how I felt about Ethan.

Maybe that was the point? He was trying to find the words to explain why it hadn't worked. Maybe he was in denial over his failure.

I flew out of there and sped back into Cameron's office and grabbed my handbag. With shaking hands I fumbled for my car keys on my way out the front door.

Rain fell and a gust of leaves blew up and around me. The Santa Ana winds were at their worst.

My car was where I'd left it—parked in Cameron's VIP spot.

A sleek limousine I'd only been vaguely aware of pulled away from the curb and idled in front of me. Of course, Cameron would know I'd come after them. He'd also know I'd be in no state to drive.

Relenting to his siren call, I climbed inside the limo.

Traffic was dense and impossible due to the heavy downpour, with a commute that would normally take an hour taking two. Neither Cameron nor Ethan answered their phones. The journey was endless and felt like the longest drive I'd ever taken.

No, not the longest…

That had been the one where Cameron had driven me away from Danton's a week after his death. There had been no consolation in knowing Danton had gone peacefully, and had been loved so completely. I'd been too torn up to believe life would even go on.

I'd never met another man like him…until Ethan.

The limo pulled into the driveway to Cameron's multi-million dollar home. The impressive estate with its imposing fountain out front was again a reminder that this was a coveted piece of real estate, even for this wealthy neighborhood. He'd had this home for a while and had once told me he'd regretted giving his gay interior designer free reign. The man had had taken the chandelier theme that Cameron was fond of and turned his house into a monument to all things crystal. Like with most things in life, Cameron never took the issue too seriously.

I went on in.

At least the masculine black and white marble floor tiles offset all the surrounding glamour. But the erotically shaped central chandelier was truly a piece of glorious art.

Ethan sat at the bottom of the staircase.

"Hey," he said.

I made my way toward him, glancing around for Cameron.

"Hi." I cupped Ethan's face and he closed his eyes. "You okay?"

"God, I missed you."

"I should have been in there."

He shook his head. "I didn't want you to see me like that."

Cameron would have taken Ethan all the way back to the beginning. Right into the eye of the storm until he'd desensitized him to the dreadful event, and in his own indomitable way he'd have purged all guilt and pain.

I rested my head on his lap and we stayed like that for a while. Ethan brushed his fingertips through my hair and it made my scalp tingle. Being with him again was all I wanted.

Finally, he stroked my back to get me to raise my head. Then he pushed himself to his feet and stared down at me. I held his gaze, conveying that he was more of a man than any I'd ever met. He was strong and brave and gorgeous and quite simply, I loved him.

He held out his hand to me and I took it, rising to my feet.

Together we made our way up the stairs. It felt so good to be close to him again, I wasn't sure how I'd endured our time apart.

The room he led me into was one I'd stayed in so many times before when visiting Cameron. This bedroom with its huge four-poster bed and dark furniture made it luxuriously cozy. The fine artwork hanging on the walls was a reminder of Cameron's incredible style.

Whatever Ethan needed, I knew how to give it intuitively.

He crushed my mouth to his, his tongue tangling with mine, a flash of fierceness in his kiss.

His erection nudged my lower abdomen.

I broke away and stared into his eyes as we shared a moment of realization.

"I'm burning up for you," he whispered.

Ripping at his shirt I told him, "Whatever you need I can take it."

Our kissing resumed and we were wild together, acting in a blaze of heat as though we'd been apart forever, his body pressed to mine, his cock growing harder.

I felt overwhelming happiness for him...for us.

My jaw dropped when I saw his enormous beautiful cock bursting out of dark curls in a tantalizing tease.

"Yeah." He gave a wide smile. "Better watch out, baby."

He threw me onto the bed and his laughter was endearing as he ripped the rest of my clothes off, pulling at my panties and easing them over my hips. He scrunched them up and brought them to his nose and breathed me in; so sensually decadent.

"You intoxicate me," he whispered, taking my nipple in his mouth, suckling, sending shockwaves of bliss straight to my sex.

Ethan's kisses trailed over my belly and went lower until he reached my clit. His tongue flicked stunning pleasure into that sensitized nub, and an orgasm rippled through me, forcing my back to arch and my breath to catch.

"Need to be inside you." He rose up and plunged into me, filling me entirely.

The lusciousness of him inside me sparked a need to bring my legs up and wrap them around him to hold him tighter.

My sex clutched at Ethan's cock, the pleasure growing to a blinding intensity.

"I'm coming again," I told him.

He slowed his pace, thrusting in and out of me leisurely. "Jesus, Scarlet, you feel incredible." Ethan squeezed his eyes shut. "Can we stay in bed forever?"

"Fine by me."

He ground his pelvis over my clit with each thrust.

"Oh, yes. Right there."

Other than our sighs, the quiet surrounded us as we savored each other, me gripping him as though refusing to ever let go again.

When he finally came, he sent me over the edge again.

He collapsed at my side. I flung my leg over his, and we drifted to sleep.

Later that evening I woke, hearing birds outside the bay window chirping away, their sweet songs making the room feel cozy.

Stretching, I looked over at Ethan who was blinking awake. He looked so beautiful, so rested, like all the tension he'd once held on to was now gone.

"Hi," I said softly.

He smiled. "Let's hope this is Hotel California."

"Silly."

Laying there with my head resting on the pillow, happy and sated, I suppressed an urge to tell Ethan just how fantastic sex was with him. I didn't want to undermine what we'd shared before, because those tender moments of intimacy had touched me just as deeply and brought us closer.

Still, my body tingled deliciously with its post-fucked lull, and I stretched leisurely, my right hand coming to rest on his bicep.

All those years ago, way back during my time in France, I'd learned the profoundness of what it was to love entirely and that with each breath, each moment of faith, my soul could sooth another's.

Being here with Ethan felt like the final journey of my authentic self, as though I'd always been destined to be by his side. Loving him completely had been inevitable, I knew that now.

He looked over at me with passion in his eyes.

I bit my lip, scared that I might say the wrong thing and ruin this moment.

"You're very quiet," he said.

I tilted my head to look at him. "You have that effect."

"That was fucking amazing." He raised his hand. "Sorry for the language but I'd forgotten how good that can feel."

"I like spending time with you, Ethan."

"Why do I sense a 'but' coming?"

"Happiness makes me nervous."

He reached out and took my hand, kissing my wrist. I melted as his soft lips caressed my skin. "I'm still here."

"Thank you for trusting me."

He arched a brow as though realizing I was talking about Chrysalis. "That might have been one of the craziest weeks of my life. I wasn't allowed out. Cameron literally locked me in there." He chuckled. "It was insane."

"But it worked."

"I'm sure you're intrigued with what happened in there?"

"It's between you and your doctor."

Ethan let out another low chuckle. "Yeah, right."

"You don't regret it, do you?"

He peeked beneath the covers at his cock. "Doesn't look like it."

My gaze followed his and I could see he was ready to go again. I tingled all over, thinking of the kind of pleasure that was imminent.

Ethan let out a sigh. "What Cameron pulled off was a goddamned miracle. And believe it or not it has little to do with this big guy here." He gestured downward.

I smiled.

"The pain that was lodged in my chest for years is gone. Completely gone. The memories are there, but Cameron did this ninja trick on the way I connect to those memories and I feel free of guilt for the first time since…"

"I'm so relieved." Rolling onto my side I rested my head on his chest. "I stayed at Chrysalis the entire time and was pacing constantly. Nearly gatecrashed your therapy."

"I'd have been like," he raised his hand, "welcome to the party. Pull up a chair. The circus is in town."

"Was it scary?"

"At first. Then, halfway through the week we just sat around eating pizza and chatting about life like we were old buddies. Until the late night sessions resumed. Richard shared his experience with me of what Cameron had done to him. I got off lightly, apparently."

"Richard lost someone close to him, too."

"He told me about his fiancée's death."

"Cameron wanted you to see it was possible."

"I'd been ignoring the symptoms for so long." He reached low and caressed his erection. "I can't believe it."

"I'm so relieved you got to see the good work we do." I cringed. "That didn't come out right. You're more to me than that."

"I get what you're saying."

I lifted my head and looked toward the door.

Ethan followed my gaze. "We won't be disturbed."

"Oh?"

"Cameron told me we can stay here all weekend if we like."

"He's not here?"

"Left before you arrived. He wanted us to have privacy."

My head crashed back onto the pillow. "We have the weekend together?"

"If you want."

I beamed at him. "I want."

"I missed you. You were my motivation. All I could think of was being able to please you, Scarlet."

Sliding down beneath the covers, I lowered myself between his thighs and then glanced up at him. His eyelids closed as I took him in my mouth. Lapping and sucking, I found the equivalent of a G-spot between where his balls met his shaft, making him writhe. To slow him down a little, I concentrated on the head of his cock, my tongue circling it until his breaths were short and sharp, and pre-cum beaded at the tip.

"Scarlet," he said. "You're a miracle worker."

Gently, I pulled on his balls and felt him go still beneath me, my other hand working him up and down in unison with my mouth.

"I'm close."

"Let me drink you."

Ethan groaned loudly, clutching at the sheets as his hips bucked, his warmth filling my mouth. I swallowed, thrilled to see him so enraptured, so carried away with bliss.

His body shuddered and he cried out.

I moved up next to him and rested my head on his chest, watching him carefully, knowing an emotional floodgate might be released at any moment.

I wanted him to know I was here for him.

"I'm going to warn you," he said. "Cameron gave me a cocktail of medications, too."

"Testosterone?"

"Shot right in my butt. Apparently my levels were low. That, and all this intensive psychotherapy has made this," he looked down, "my new superpower. Watch out lady, I'm going to be taking you every five minutes."

"Oh, really?" I grinned at him.

He stared up at the ceiling. "I think I'm going to marry you."

"Ethan…"

"Was that wrong of me?"

I crashed onto him and he hugged me tightly. "All I can think of is making you happy."

CHAPTER 27

E THAN WANTED TO SEE CAMERON'S HOUSE.
After sharing a long, hot shower, we'd both dressed and
made our way down to the ground floor.

I led Ethan down to the ridiculously large kitchen. The luxurious space could have been lifted out of a home in Tuscany. Of course, I knew it intimately from all those parties I'd attended—everyone had always ended up hanging out here. It had an Italian flair, with blue and yellow tiles, highlighted by the light streaming in through the large windows.

Ethan perched on one of the tall barstools and leaned his elbows on the black granite countertop, watching me. I set about preparing us some lemon water in two tall crystal glasses filled with ice. Rummaging through Cam's fridge, I found us a selection of stuffed olives and pâté and crackers.

This house really did feel like home. Cameron was the brother I'd never had and he always made everyone feel welcome—even when he wasn't here. His generosity knew no bounds.

Refreshed, we left the kitchen and headed down the west hallway, both of us pausing here and there to admire the many paintings lining the walls. It was fun to take a moment to contemplate the undertones of each one.

Captured within a simple black frame was a painting of a young virgin running away from a winged angel. The oil colors were extraordinary and caught the light in the most exquisite way. It made me wonder if Cameron had bought this one because in some way he was working through some ideology. He was, after all, considered a connoisseur of the dark arts and was a man who liked his sex with extra-kink and a healthy layer of love.

He knew all too well he had the ability to mind-fuck a woman into obsessing over him night and day, so he always chose his lovers carefully—too carefully, as far as I was concerned.

I so wanted him to find that special someone. The last woman in Cam's life, McKenzie Carter, had almost destroyed him and it made me wonder whether he'd ever risk his heart again.

Ethan pointed to a door. "What's in here?"

"Have a look." I gestured for him to open it.

We stepped onto the hardwood floor of the gym.

"He fences in here," I told him. "Shay taught him, but in true Cameron fashion—"

"He outgrew his teacher?"

"You could say that."

Ethan scrunched up his nose. "Is there anything Cole can't do?"

"I'm still figuring that out."

"Bet he can't do this." Ethan jogged over toward the back of the room and picked up the lone basketball resting against the wall. He bounced it a few times and then threw it high into the net above—a slam dunk.

He cheered as though he'd just defeated the entire Lakers' team.

I moved quickly toward him. "I've been known to land a few shots myself."

"Really?" He arched a brow and threw the ball over to me.

I caught it, then circled beneath the net, leaped up and tossed the ball right in. Jumping up and down, I cheered like I'd thrown the winning shot.

Ethan pumped his fist in the air.

We played a little longer and it was fun to relax and forget everything for a while.

Leaving the gym, we headed out to the sprawling garden. Tall lush trees lined the high walls to ensure privacy. Tiles from Rome had been shipped in to decorate the sparkling pool in the center, where I had enjoyed swimming so many times in the past.

Ethan looked impressed. "I'm surprised Cameron ever leaves this place."

"I know, right?"

"Yeah, medicine is not paying for this place."

"He's a Cole."

Ethan shrugged. "Which means?"

"Cole Tea. Tempest Coffee."

Ethan's expression changed to awe as his gaze swept over the garden. "It's his dad's company?"

"I thought you knew."

"No, I dug around for information on him but only his clinic came up. Everything I found online about Cameron was positive. I'm assuming that's partially thanks to Shay."

"Cam is squeaky clean." I raised my hand in defense of the statement. "He doesn't do drugs. He donates to charity. He's good to women, and his staff loves him. He's honest and kind."

"All right, all right, but…come on. Let me in on one of his weaknesses."

I let out a deep sigh. "We're his weakness, Ethan. His friends. He'd do anything for us."

"There must be something? Some scandal?"

"He had his heart broken by a woman not that long ago."

"What happened?"

"He's also very private." I walked over to the edge of the pool and knelt, dipping my hand in the warm water. "It's heated. Wanna take a dip?"

"Actually, I have an appointment."

"Tonight?"

"Yes. Visiting rights."

"Oh?"

"I have a baby. She's my pride and joy. Just eight weeks old." He came over and knelt beside me, smiling. "Want to meet her?"

My jaw had fallen open, and I slammed it shut.

"A baby?" I was trying to process this revelation while I studied his face for the truth.

"She's adopted."

There were so many issues to contend with, not the least of which was that his life had been under threat—and anyone connected to him was also at risk. Had he really placed a baby in jeopardy?

"You look surprised."

"A little, maybe. I'd love to meet her though."

He pushed himself to his feet.

I tried to keep my concern from showing. "Where is she?"

"Secret location."

I stood and stared up at him. "I'd like to come with you."

I was having so much fun with him, the thought of parting was too painful right now—and there was something intriguing about seeing him with a baby.

A fricken baby! Ethan Neilson, Mr. Hard Ass! My mind was blown.

"Shit, I just realized," he said. "I don't have my car."

"Oh, no, neither do I!"

"We can grab a taxi. Or an Uber?"

"I have an idea. Come on."

A few minutes later, Ethan was left speechless. We stood in Cameron's subterranean parking structure right beneath the house.

His twenty-car collection was impressive, and included a Bugatti Veyron, a Porsche Spyder and a well-preserved Mustang.

"He has a Corvette Z06?" Ethan practically drooled. "Zero to sixty in less than three seconds."

The blue sports car he was giddy over really was a thing of beauty with its sleek lines and low chassis.

"We'll take the Corvette then." I headed back to the wall safe.

"No way."

"I borrow his cars all the time."

"This isn't right, Scarlet. It's one thing to stay in his house."

I opened the safe and pulled out the keys to the Corvette, then dangled them in front of him. "Are you sure?"

He stepped back as though hating the idea.

"Come on," I said. "It'll be fun."

"Call him."

"You call him."

"I'm not calling him and asking to borrow one of his cars. He'll really think I'm taking advantage."

I pulled out my phone and checked the bars finding the signal weak, but usable. I slid my finger over to my contacts and pressed Cameron's number.

"Hey," Cam answered quickly. "How's it going?"

"Hello, my darling," I said brightly. "Everything is amazing. Can you tell Ethan we can borrow your Corvette?"

He laughed. "Sure."

I beamed and handed Ethan my phone.

"Cameron," Ethan began, "I appreciate you letting me stay here. You've gone above and beyond and I can't thank you enough."

He listened intently to Cameron for a minute or so.

"You don't have to do that," Ethan said, combing his fingers through his hair. "You've already—"

I gave Ethan a thumbs-up in anticipation.

"I feel like I'm imposing. Are you sure, Cameron?"

When the call ended, Ethan turned to face the car, his expression full of wonder. "Well, fuck me."

"I'm driving." I headed on over to the Corvette.

He followed. "No, Cameron specifically told me I was to drive."

"Who's the boss here?"

"That's me. Most definitely."

I melted at his cheeky grin and the way he ran his fingers over the sleek hood.

But I still hid the keys behind my back.

He tackled me for them and I tried to stay upright. I'd not laughed this hard in years.

CHAPTER 28

THE CORVETTE DROVE LIKE A DREAM WITH ETHAN AT THE wheel.

Wearing a big smile, he weaved the sports car through heavy traffic. We slowed when we reached the 134 Freeway. My gaze drifted over to Providence Saint Joseph's Hospital, looming large to our right.

We drove past its freeway exit.

I looked at Ethan. "Are we going to someone's home?"

"No."

"Where then?"

"You'll figure it out."

"Did you use a surrogate?" The thought of another woman carrying Ethan's child made me examine my feelings. It would have been his DNA growing in her womb. I flinched when my fingernails dug too deeply into my palms.

"You're a bit nosy, aren't you?" He revved the engine and slid into the right lane.

Ethan was having a little too much fun. He seemed overly excited about seeing his baby, and the more I thought about it the more it made sense to me.

I'd never met anyone I wanted to have a child with until now. I'd pushed that dream behind me. My thoughts ran wild with the possibility of becoming a loving stepmother to Ethan's baby girl. I'd really try and get to know her. I promised myself that.

He steered us off Victoria Avenue and we made a right turn followed by a quick left.

And then I saw the sign and my jaw tightened.

No, he didn't just do this to me...

"Ethan," I snapped.

He turned the radio up and Queen's "Somebody to Love" blared from the speakers.

Although I sensed what was coming it was hard to be angry with Ethan for long.

We pulled into the parking lot of the L.A. Zoo.

"Ethan?" I nudged his ribs.

"You know what they say about people who assume," he said with a grin. He climbed out of the car and ran round to my side.

He opened my door in a gallant fashion. That "southern gentleman" act of his always made me smile.

I accepted his hand. "You're a cheeky bastard."

He laughed and led me toward the front gate. With a flash of his ID, which he'd slipped out of his wallet, we were through and heading up the wide expanse to the interior of the park. The scent of green grass and animal dung wafted through the air as we strolled hand in hand. I didn't mind the smells—I liked the earthiness of it all.

"This place closes at 5:00 P.M., so most of the animals are bedded down for the night. Stand here a minute, I want to take a photo of you." He nudged me up against a fence and I smiled for him.

Ethan held his iPhone steady. "I'm filming you."

I waved and said, "It's our day out at the zoo. We're here to see Ethan's baby. I can't wait."

He kept filming. "You are one brave lady."

"What?"

"Look behind you."

I turned to see a chain-link fence and behind it was a swampy pond. I saw the tail first.

A ten-foot alligator.

"Jesus Christ—" I leaped toward Ethan.

He howled and tried to fight off my fists as I struck him playfully.

I braved another look at the alligator. It was merely soaking up the last rays of the sun, lying eerily still and camouflaged amongst all the foliage.

"I'll make it up to you." Ethan pulled me along eagerly.

Ethan used his ID again to gain us entry into a large building. After pushing through a few doors we ended up in a long corridor.

We peered through the wide glass window of what looked like a nursery. Several incubators were lined up side by side.

I laughed with utter joy. "This is her?"

"This is her." He gave a wave to a small white monkey with a pink face. She was on the lap of an employee who was sitting in a rocking chair, bottle feeding her.

Ethan really did look like a proud father.

"How did you happen to adopt a monkey?" I said, my face aching from a ridiculous smile.

"Adoptions help fund the animals' care. The zoo and botanical gardens are owned by the City, and even with thousands of visitors it's an expensive place to run." He pointed at the baby monkey. "Poppy was abandoned so we're bottle feeding her. We'll try and integrate her back with her mom as soon as possible."

"So, no taking her home then?" I nudged his arm.

"I wish. She's a colobus monkey. From Kenya."

"You really are full of surprises, Ethan."

He shrugged. "I enjoy hanging out here. All the staff are laid-back and happy. And of course I know the argument about how it's cruel to keep animals locked up, but they're safe here and well looked after. No predators."

I couldn't keep my eyes off Poppy, the way she happily nursed her bottle, the way her gaze stayed on the employee who was feeding her.

"Let's get you into a sterile gown," he said.

"I can feed her?"

"That's why we're here."

Oh, my god.

Within several minutes I'd washed my hands, pulled on non-latex gloves, and was wearing a white disposable gown.

Once I was settled in the rocking chair, Ethan placed Poppy on my lap and showed me how to hold her. With his expert guidance, I held the bottle of milk to Poppy's lips and she latched on to the teat, taking it all the way into her mouth, her small hands gripping mine.

I'd never been this close to anything this cute before. Her soft fur tickled my hands, and her large brown eyes stared trustingly into mine.

"Ethan, you have a magical side." I looked up at him.

He gave me a gentle smile.

"I can add your name to the adoption papers, if you like." He kissed the top of my head. "Happiness suits you."

CHAPTER 29

"ARE YOU SURE?" ASKED SHAY.

He leaned back against my kitchen counter, his gaze fixed on mine.

This man had seen combat as a Navy SEAL. He'd kept his fitness up and his hard muscled physique hadn't lost any of its gorgeousness.

I was proud to call him one of my closest friends.

"I'm fine." I gave him a warm smile as proof. "Ethan's gone to get a carton of cream." I stirred the pot of bolognaise and then rested the wooden spoon on a small plate. "I've been a little ditzy lately and forgot it when we went shopping."

"We?"

"Me and Ethan."

"Sounds cozy."

I smirked "You're still my number one man, Shay."

"Other than Cameron?"

"A love like no other."

He arched a brow. "I think I'm feeling jealous."

"Of Cameron?"

"Ethan."

I folded my arms across my chest. "Very funny. You're with Arianna."

He looked away.

"How is she?"

"Fine." His gaze met mine. "You and me, we could have been a thing."

"Only I'd be on top, Shay. I like to be in control."

"Ethan's a dom."

"He's a switch." I suppressed a smile knowing full well that Shay was also, only he'd never admitted it and had never played out his fantasy. His alpha pride went too deep. And so far, he'd never confessed his adorable crush on Cameron.

He walked over to my fridge and reached in for a beer. "Want one?"

I waved it off, happy he felt so at home here. "We're having wine."

Shay found the bottle opener and worked on leveraging the top. "Which brings me to the reason I'm here."

"Oh?"

"It can't go on, Scarlet."

My back straightened and I went over and turned down the heat under the pot of bolognaise.

"Hear me out," he said.

"Did Cameron send you?"

"I'm head of security. It's my job to keep you safe. Keep everyone safe."

"The man who tried to kill Ethan is dead."

"When the cartel can't find their hit man, they'll connect the dots. Don't be naive." He came closer and tipped up my chin. "Ethan is still in danger."

"Are you telling me we can't be friends?"

Shay grabbed my shoulder. "That's exactly what I'm staying."

I tried to break free, but his grip was too strong.

"Scarlet?"

"We'll be careful."

He blinked, looking annoyed. "Do you want me to tell him to stay away?"

"No." Again I tried to twist out of his grasp.

His strength overwhelmed mine.

"I love you, Scar." He loosened his grip. "We all do. When the cartel comes for Ethan, and they will—"

"Don't." I broke away and turned my back on him.

A thousand scenarios flashed through my brain and they were all too painful to contemplate.

"I hate doing this to you. You know I do."

"You can stay for dinner if you like. There's more than enough. Go set the table."

He took a sip of beer. "Ethan shot a man at point blank range. And he just got out of a weeklong session with our good doctor. Ethan's not thinking straight."

"What are you insinuating? That I'm taking advantage?"

"You owe him nothing."

"Only my life."

"You feel you need to repay him?"

"You think that's why we're together?"

"You're still fucking him?" He frowned. "That was treatment-based therapy. You're off the reservation."

"He needs me. He hasn't loved anyone since his wife died."

"Love?"

"Fuck off, Shay. Go do what it is you do. Go protect Chrysalis from the real threats that are out there."

He set his beer on the countertop and sauntered over to me. He nudged me back against the wall and pressed his body against mine, towering over me.

"Excuse me?" He looked pissed off.

"Let me have this," I whispered. "Ethan's all I want. Just him."

"This is your last date with him. It's over."

"No."

"This is my nice side. Don't make me show you my dark side."

"You actually think you can boss me around?" I shoved at him but it was useless, he was too damn strong.

"I call the shots, Scarlet. Cameron's given me full authority. You know that. So do as you're told. Stop making my job fucking harder."

Ethan meant so much to me, the kind of connection I'd not experienced since...

No, don't think of Danton now, not when Shay needs to see my iron will.

"Every day threats are coming in. You don't see them because that's how Cameron wants it. You're protected from all the annoying details."

"Like?"

"Death threats against Cameron. Against others at the club."

My breath stuttered. "Have there been any against me?"

He lowered his gaze, giving me my answer.

"What happened?" I muttered. "Who—"

"That's where I come in. So you don't have to know."

Shay was Cameron's corporate bad boy and he had always been able to protect us. And in truth none of us had really wanted to know the intimate details of what it took to ensure Chrysalis and Enthrall remained safe and its employees unscathed.

"Baby," Shay said softly, his mouth brushing mine. "Don't fight me. Let me protect you."

"I'm going to keep him."

He smiled. "No, you're not."

I grazed my teeth over my bottom lip.

"God, you're so damn fuckable, Scarlet."

"Well, this is awkward." It was Ethan.

He stood in the doorway, blinking at us in confusion.

Shay stepped back.

"Ethan—" I stepped toward him. "It's not what it looks like, please."

He held up the carton of cream. "I think this is what you wanted me to get for you. Conveniently." He glared at Shay. "God, I'm slow to catch on."

"We're not together," I used the last air in my lungs in a panic. "Shay was checking on me. That's all."

Ethan looked so hurt; a dreadful pain reflected in his eyes.

"You being here places her in danger." Shay narrowed his gaze on him. "You know this."

Ethan shrugged. "The heart wants what the heart wants."

I sucked in a breath. "Oh, Ethan."

"Get police protection," said Shay. "So no one else gets hurt."

Ethan closed his eyes for a second. "Let me take a wild guess. This was the master plan all along. Seduce me into the club so that I'm so far down the rabbit hole there's no way back for me. Chrysalis is safe and you are all free to go on with your lives."

"No." I stepped closer. "That's not it at all."

His gaze snapped to mine. "I thought we had something special, Scarlet?"

"We do. We are."

He bowed his head and turned on his heel, heading for the door.

"Wait!" I went after him.

Shay grabbed my arm. "Let him go."

"No, not like this."

Shay maneuvered behind me and captured my arms by my side, holding me still. "This is for the best."

"He loves me. I'm the only thing he has to live for!"

"Scarlet, he has a cartel crosshair on his forehead."

I yanked free. "You may have Arianna, but you don't know true love."

He gave a shrug. "I'm still alive."

"Do you have any idea how much you just hurt him?"

"Let this go, Scarlet. Disobedience won't be tolerated by us. We set the rules."

"Don't talk to me like that," I snapped. "Remember who I am."

"That's why I do what I do," he said gently. "To protect you at any cost. Because you're Scarlet Winters, and no one else comes close to how incredible you are."

"Did Cameron send you?"

"Take a wild guess." He headed for the door.

"Tell him he's overstepped his mark this time."

"Cole's given you the week off. Take the time to decompress. Analyze what's really going on here. You've got a crush on a client. That's all this is."

The door slammed behind him.

In a daze, I strolled into the living room and walked right over to my beloved cello. Kneeling before it, I rested my forehead against the curve of the wood.

I tried to remember how to breathe.

CHAPTER 30

T HERE WAS NO OTHER WAY I WAS GOING TO SURVIVE THIS separation from Ethan.

I was too far gone—blinded by desire so deeply that I refused to consider the risks of being with him. Yes, I'd been naive but I'd been so happy in my hours of denial. This week of no contact with him had felt like an eternity.

What hurt most was Ethan refusing to take my calls. I needed to explain to him that Shay and I had never been intimate, but more importantly, I wanted to tell him his treatment had been executed with nothing but respect.

I did the only thing I knew how to do to start getting over him. I gave the finger to all those alpha males with too much time on their hands.

I went mother-fucking shopping.

That's right, bitches. I brought the corporate Chrysalis credit card with me and laid down some serious cash on the sucker.

Why, thank you for all my goodies I've just purchased, Dr. Cameron Cole.

Interfering bastard.

Just because you don't want me to end up in some cartel scandal and wind up dead doesn't mean you can interfere in my life.

It was time for chocolate.

Sitting in the corner of Beranger's Café in Pacific Palisades, I ordered up a double chocolate milkshake with vanilla ice cream—with a ton of whipped cream on top, too.

Sweet revenge, fuckers.

I peeked inside my Louis Vuitton shopping bag and admired my new bright pink Alma BB's, and then reached for the bag containing my brand new Christian Louboutin Ombre crystal pumps. Lifting the lid to the box, I swooned at the twinkling Swarovski crystals that made these shoes ironically a man trap. Anyone with a foot fetish would come in his pants if he saw these.

Chocolate and a splash of color would put a bounce back in my step.

Right.

I was miserable. I tried rubbing my chest to soothe my aching heart.

My iPhone buzzed and I pressed it to my ear.

"Mistress Scarlet?" said Cameron.

"Yes, *Master* Cole?" I laid on the sarcasm.

"So what did you buy?"

"Actually, I'm at a movie."

"What are you seeing?"

"Um…"

I leaned forward and sucked on my straw. The shake tasted amazing, titillating my taste buds with milky, chocolaty goodness.

"That latest blockbuster…*New Shoes*?" he asked.

"Are you following me?"

"I've known you a long time."

"FYI, I'm over this romance shit."

"Really?"

"The pursuit of happily ever after." I peeked at my treasures again.

"Well, well, and cream, too?"

I narrowed my gaze when it landed on the dashing Cameron Cole. He was standing on the other side of the shop's front window with his phone pressed to his ear. He threw me a wave and headed on in through the door.

He made his way over to my corner table.

Cameron beamed when he saw my shopping bags. "Last time you went on a bender with my American Express card you racked up a one hundred thousand dollar bill. Looks like you've lost your edge."

"Thank you for my new shoes."

He smirked and rounded the table to sit beside me.

The waitress came over.

Cameron glanced at the menu. "I would have what she's having only I seem to have forgotten my insulin," he joked. "Earl Grey, please."

The waitress hurried off, blushing wildly. This stunning alpha male always had the girls swooning.

"So, how are you?" He dragged my milkshake over to him and took a sip. "Okay, wow. This being a 'broken woman' thing has its privileges."

"Fuck you."

"Love you."

"Do you want to see the shoes you bought me?"

"Sure." He peeked in and cringed. "Those are going back."

"I like them."

"They're a bit shiny."

"You're not the one who'll be wearing them."

"Good point. They look like happy shoes."

"They are happy shoes. They're 'the world can go fuck itself' shoes."

"You really love him?"

"Who?"

"He's complicated."

"So am I."

"Yes, but you don't have any evil men hunting you down."

"I haven't felt this way since…"

"Danton was special."

"Too special. He ruined me for all other men."

"You've never told me you hate me for what I had you do for him."

"You mean being with Danton during his final months?" I sighed deeply. "Those were the happiest days of my life. You made that happen, Cameron. Danton changed my life. Good God, he saved it."

And Cameron had saved it, too, by sending me to him.

He gave me a kind smile. "Danton told me it was the happiest time of his life too. Considering what he was going through that was quite an admission. You know how much he adored you."

"His love will last a lifetime." Tears stung my eyes, but I forced them back. "Do you think…?"

"Go on."

"When Ethan heard the cello playing, do you think it really was Danton getting a message to me?"

Cameron stared down at his hands. "Why not, Scarlet? He promised he'd come to you if you ever needed him."

Yes, he had…those were the last words he'd spoken, his promise to always watch over me.

"The thing is," I continued softly, "I felt him."

He nodded. "There you are then."

The waitress delivered his Earl Grey and Cameron grinned when he noticed the "Cole" logo on the tea tag.

It made me smile, too. Our waitress had no idea that Cameron came from the billion dollar empire that was Cole Tea. It was best if things stayed that way. If him being one of the most beautiful men in the world didn't overwhelm you, finding out he was also a billionaire was a shock like no other.

He deserved to be happy. To find "the one."

Maybe if Cameron fell for someone he'd leave the rest of us alone and we could all get on with fucking up our own lives again.

I turned to face him. "Ethan is brilliant and sexy and feisty and so handsome."

Cameron arched a brow. "I was just thinking that."

"I love him."

"He's cracked your ice-dragon demeanor. That's quite an accomplishment."

"He's kind and patient and he gets me."

"Well, that's good."

"And he has a monkey baby." It came out in a rush.

"Do I even want to know what that means?"

I rubbed my tired eyes. "He adopted a baby monkey at the L.A. Zoo and I got to meet her. Her name's Poppy. He has visiting rights and everything."

Cameron smirked. "Even worse than I thought."

I took a long sip of my chocolate shake and then slid the glass over to Cameron. "You work miracles. Can't you do something to make this happen for me?"

He sighed. "I have this wild, brilliant plan."

I perked up. "Oh?"

"Richard's spiraling again."

My shoulders slumped. I was disappointed that he'd changed the subject. "How?"

He gestured he wasn't going to expand on the matter. "I want us to start looking for a submissive that'll be a perfect fit for him. It'll take time. But keep your eyes out for someone special. We'll save her from banality and give her a glorious life."

"You know how arrogant that sounds, right?"

"She'll succumb with full consent."

"Rascal. So, have you a personality type in mind?"

"Pure innocence. Someone he'll want to protect. Someone who will breech his badass defenses. A subject with a damaged past. She'll keep him distracted and busy as he tries to figure her out. Let's go for stunning. Breathtaking. Pure fuckable material."

"I'll throw a dinner party for us. How about that? So we can chat about it."

"Sure. But we won't be telling Richard our plan."

It was my turn to roll my eyes.

My phone buzzed and I stared at the screen.

"I'll ignore it." I showed Cameron it was Ethan.

"Take it."

"I'm allowed?" I pouted at him.

"Sure."

After hesitating, I answered the call.

"Hello...Scarlet?" Ethan's southern drawl rippled through me, reaching my soul, making me want to swoon. It was hard to think straight as a sense of loss caused my chest to tighten.

"I know you're there," he said, his tone tense.

"Hello, Ethan."

"How are you?"

"Oh, fine."

"Really?"

It was too much. I couldn't do this, couldn't hear his voice and know our time was over and drag this out. "I can't talk now."

"Visit me at my office. We need to discuss an issue."

"What issue?"

"You have the address? From the time you followed me home after spying on me?"

"What day is good for you? I'll check my calendar."

"Now."

"That's actually inconvenient—"

"Within the hour. Or I'll have you arrested and brought to my office."

"Will it involve handcuffs?"

He went silent.

I caught Cameron arching his eyebrows questioningly.

"See you soon then." Ethan ended the call.

I lowered my phone and held Cameron's gaze. "He wants to see me."

"Give him my regards."

"Come with me?"

Cameron took a sip of tea. "You're Scarlet Winters. You'll handle him just fine."

"What do you think he wants?"

"Knowing Neilson, the last word, probably."

Facing off with him would be terrifying—for no other reason than I still loved him.

CHAPTER 31

E THAN'S SECRETARY PEERED DOWN AT HER BOSS'S appointment book.

It made me smile a little that she still used this old-fashioned way of keeping track of his schedule. It almost took my mind off why I was here.

This meeting was probably arranged to warn me of his impending lawsuit against us, though Cameron had reassured me the non-disclosure agreement that he had Ethan sign pre-therapy was watertight.

His secretary looked like the kind of woman a D.A. would need to stop the riffraff from disrupting his day—a bright Hispanic with graying temples and a no-nonsense attitude.

"Mr. Neilson made the appointment himself," I explained.

"I did," he said. "Thank you, Edith."

I turned round and saw him standing there, all edgy D.A., and wearing a snazzy dark suit. It was hard to read his expression. He looked like he'd been working out, his tan had deepened, too, and he'd gotten a haircut.

God, he really did look gorgeous.

I raised my chin proudly. "I don't have much time."

"Come in." He gestured to his office. "Glad you could make it."

I forced myself to smile at his secretary.

Ethan looked over to her. "Hold all calls, please."

"Of course, Mr. Neilson. Would you like coffee?"

"Not yet, thank you."

I avoided eye contact with him as I slipped past him into his office. A fancy framed law certificate with his name embossed in gold hung on the wall by his desk. The room's décor was simple—though the numerous stacks of papers scattered here and there made it look a little like organized chaos.

Ethan's gaze stayed on me and I felt too fragile right now for an argument. His gorgeous good looks and that southern drawl had my body betraying me.

My sex clenched and my nipples hardened.

"It's cold in here." I hoped he'd believe me.

He gave me a smug little smile, no doubt sensing my arousal.

I folded my arms across my chest. "I have another appointment. Can we cut to the chase, Mr. Neilson?"

His jaw tensed. He strolled back over to the door and locked it.

"How have you been, Ms. Winters?" He turned to face me and moved leisurely around to the other side of his desk, his hands now casually tucked into his pants pockets.

"I'm glad we got this time to talk," I said breathlessly. "I wanted to explain—"

He raised his hand to cut me off. "No need."

"I want to leave on good terms, Ethan."

I needed to know he'd forgiven me for any pain I'd unwittingly caused him. I couldn't go on with this tension between us. Not after everything we'd shared.

The way his gaze swept over me caused me to feel another sharp pang of regret.

He held his hand out for me and I moved toward him. He grabbed my wrist and pulled me around to his side.

This. I was not expecting this…

Perhaps a berating, or an outburst of anger over how betrayed he felt.

Yet Ethan's eyes burned with a raw passion. As he pushed me up against his desk I caught a glimpse of a wry smile. He turned me to face the desk and nudged me forward, bending me over it. My heart missed a beat when I felt him edge up the hem of my skirt. His hands squeezed my butt cheeks.

I let out a gasp of pleasure.

His hand slapped my ass. "You will remain silent, understand?" "Yes."

Ethan grabbed my shoulders and pulled me upright. He spun me around and lifted me up to sit on the edge of his desk. My heart was hammering away—being this close to him again was destroying me. Breathing in his sexy cologne, that intoxicating scent of spices, threw my self-assurance off balance.

Those strong hands of his were now hiking up my pencil skirt, and I lifted my butt to help him, marveling at how we had found our way back to this.

This.

A passionate intimacy.

Ethan gently pushed me back until I was lying on his desk. Then he reached for my thong. When it was halfway down my legs he ripped it off in frustration.

He positioned himself between my thighs. "Glad you could make it, Ms. Winters. There's something we need to discuss."

"I'm listening."

He leaned low and buried his face between my thighs, letting out a moan of contentment as he suckled my clit, hungrily kissing me there, needy and vengeful in the way he flicked his tongue over my pussy.

My breathing had gotten ragged. "Ethan?"

He smiled against me. "It's either this or the slammer for the night."

"This." I grinned through my pleasure. "Oh, my God. I'm going to..."

I shuddered as his tongue began fucking my vagina, causing my thighs to shake. I tried to remember not to scream.

Ethan's hands reached up for my breasts and he cupped them, tweaking my nipples and sending me over the edge.

I slapped my hand over my mouth when the tip of his tongue circled my entrance while his fingertips played with my clit.

"I can't bear to be apart from you," I gasped out, writhing. I was wishing with all my heart this was his way of telling me we could be with each other again.

Ethan stood up straight and reached for his zipper. He pulled out his cock and it stiffened into a gorgeous erection.

He slowly slipped inside me as his face lit up with pleasure. "I missed you, Scarlet." He crushed his lips to mine. "No one will ever come close to you."

He began a perfect rhythm, thrusting in and out of me, bringing me closer still with a pleasure that was all-consuming.

I wrapped my thighs around his waist. "I'm in charge."

"Sure." He smirked. "Keep telling yourself that."

"I'll switch for you now and again. But I'm the boss."

"Hell, no, I'll switch for you. Maybe." He grinned. "If you're lucky."

"Oh, really." I squeezed him and held him firmly.

"Oh, God, Scarlet, that feels fucking amazing. You're so damn tight."

"Say 'please' before you come." I narrowed my gaze on him.

His face relaxed as he neared the edge. "We'll agree to disagree."

"I'm close."

"Come, baby. I want to feel you orgasm around my cock."

He sent me reeling into another blinding climax, my core the center of my universe as he came hard inside me, his heat sending me into an exquisite freefall as we came together, gripping each other as though nothing could keep us apart.

Time fell away as we basked in the afterglow, both of us staring at each other in awe of what had just happened.

With my head lifted off the table slightly, I watched Ethan reach for a tissue and lovingly clean between my thighs. This intimacy reminded me of all I'd lost.

Finally, he tucked himself away.

Despite everything, he couldn't regret having met me, could he?

He pulled me up and held me in a hug.

I rested my head on his shoulder. "We're still friends?"

"Most certainly hope so, after all that."

I pulled away slightly and cupped his face with my hands. "You've changed your mind about us?"

He pushed a button on his phone. "We'll take that coffee now, Edith."

"Yes, sir," came her chirpy reply.

He helped me off his desk and tugged my skirt down.

Ethan swept up my thong from the floor and tucked it into his jacket pocket.

"Consolation prize," he said, grinning wickedly.

"There's a kinky side to you, Mr. Neilson."

"Looks like you've unleashed the beast."

I giggled. "It's so good to see you."

We walked over to the two armchairs in the corner and sat opposite each other. He reached for the remote that was resting on the glass table and turned on the walled TV screen.

A blonde female NBC newscaster was reporting an incident that had occurred just this morning. There was footage playing to accompany her story—gruesome images of corpses being wheeled out of an L.A. house, all of them in body bags.

It made my stomach churn.

"Watch," he said sharply.

I gazed up at the screen again. The newscaster was discussing the deaths of a drug lord along with all his lieutenants.

I stared at Ethan.

"All of them are dead," he confirmed.

"How?"

He just looked at me for the longest time.

I slapped a hand to my mouth and stared up at the footage of a house surrounded by policemen and others with bulletproof vests stamped with D.E.A.

Ethan used the remote to lower the sound. "Shay Gardner paid me a visit."

"What? Why?"

"He told me you're not together. Nor have you ever been."

"No, never."

My attention returned to the TV screen and I couldn't help but wonder if what I was seeing was Shay's doing.

"Scarlet?"

I shook my head as I held his gaze. "You don't think that…?" I knew better than to finish that sentence.

"And I thought the cartel were dangerous," he said. "Who the fuck are you people?"

"This is not us." But I knew that Shay's loyalty to Cameron meant he'd even risk his own life.

But had they really conspired to save Ethan's?

Was this Cameron's promise to Danton coming full circle? That he would protect me at any cost and do everything in his power to make me happy?

"Ethan." I clutched the armrests to keep my hands from shaking. "What do you want from me?"

"The truth."

"About what?"

"You're in a lot of trouble, Scarlet."

"You don't have any proof that's connected to us."

"Actually, I do."

"What, exactly?"

"Shay admitted to taking care of my problem." He took my hand. "So I own your balls now, Scarlet Winters."

I stuttered out a breath. "What are you going to do?"

"Invite you away for a romantic weekend," he said, beaming. "Just you and me…if you like?"

I jumped into his lap. "Yes, oh yes, I want that."

"Cameron wanted me to know how far he'd go to protect us. He made that quite clear. Apparently he needs someone with my certain set of skills to join his team."

"You're one of us now?"

He crushed his lips to mine. "All I care about is that I get to be with you, and keep you. Do you want that?"

"I promise to make you happy."

"Then come away with me."

CHAPTER 32

E THAN'S VOICE SOUNDED TENSE.
I closed my suitcase, having unpacked my clothes neatly in our luxury suite at the Grand Colonial, our gorgeous hideaway in La Jolla. We had driven down here this evening, and I was still getting used to Ethan being with me again.

My face ached from all the smiling.

Moving closer to the bathroom, I wondered who he was on the phone with. I peaked around the door.

And froze.

He was talking into the hairdryer!

Ethan raised a finger to keep me quiet. "I can't talk now. I'm currently with the most beautiful woman in the world. I'm going to completely spoil her. No interruptions. No, I'm not telling you where I am." He caught my gaze and playfully rolled his eyes as though annoyed with the fake caller.

I leaned on the door frame and folded my arms, amused with his antics.

"Plans?" he continued. "Well, we're thinking of taking long walks

on the beach. Swimming in the heated pool. Enjoy some fine din-
ing along with lots of wild fucking." He smiled at me. "Okay, Mom,
talk to you later."

I squealed with delight as Ethan hung the hairdryer back on
the wall. He came at me fast and swept me up, carrying me into the
bedroom. He threw me onto our king-sized bed and leaped on me,
kissing me tenderly.

"Let's swim," I said.

"Anything that involves seeing you half-naked."

"Two can play at that game."

We tumbled around on the bed and slipped into a glorious round
of fucking, neither of us capable of keeping our hands off each other.

The afternoon was spent by the pool beneath large umbrellas as
we dozed away on loungers. Ethan sipped bourbon and I ordered up
my favorite cocktail, a Long Island iced tea.

When the buzz from the booze wore off I dived into the deep
end of the pool and swam its full length. When I came up for air,
Ethan was sitting on the edge. He lowered himself into the water
and pulled me into a hug.

Resting my head against his chest, I reveled in our happiness.

"We should talk," he said, his tone serious.

"About?"

"You and me. As we're in a serious relationship now I'm assuming you'll give up being a dominatrix?"

I rested my hands on his chest and nudged him back a little.
"What?"

He held my gaze. "You're not going to be alone in a room with
another man ever again. Not like that. Those days are over, Scarlet."

"What are you talking about?"

"I make more than enough money for both of us."

"You've seen what we achieve at Chrysalis. It's a therapy-based
practice. You're testament to what we can achieve—"

"That was Cameron—"

"I have clients, too. People I care about—"

"You're not gonna do this. Not when we've risked so much to get here." He glared at me. "Not after Shay put his fucking life on the line so we could be together."

"Give up being a D.A."

He pulled back more. "Don't be ridiculous."

"My job is just as important."

"I'm not sucking the dicks of my clients."

I turned sharply and pushed away, needing to get out of the pool.

"Scarlet." He grabbed me around the waist. "Wait, please. I'm sorry."

"Let me go."

"I need you to see it from my point of view."

"Ethan, I mean it."

"Jesus, Scarlet." His arms slipped from me. "Don't do this."

"Do what?" I snapped my head back.

"Run away from us."

"You've made your opinion quite clear." I gripped the hand railing of the steps and climbed up, my chest heavy from what he was asking of me.

I swept up my towel and wrapped it around me. I didn't even bother to put on my flip-flops. I merely grabbed my iPhone and room key and trudged out of the pool area and through the sliding door of the hotel.

I rode the elevator alone.

Hurrying into our suite, I grabbed my suitcase and threw it onto the bed. With shaking hands, I began to grab my stuff out of the drawers and pack.

The door flew open and Ethan stormed toward me. "You're not serious?"

I emptied the last of the drawers and slammed my case lid shut.

"Scarlet, look at me."

"We've both benefited from this."

He stepped closer. "I've never loved anyone the way I love you. And I am jealous and possessive and I know it's wrong of me to ask this of you."

I closed my eyes and said softly, "You loved your wife."

"Don't make me say it."

I whipped my head around. "I get it. Every other woman will remain in her shadow."

He looked stricken.

"Am I right?"

"She was having an affair."

I froze.

"Bastard came to her funeral." He shook his head. "Found out after the fact. Was looking at her phone to make sure I'd informed her friends and hadn't missed anyone. I found their texts, the endless messages. Her lover worked at the hospital with her. He was a surgeon."

"Oh, Ethan."

"Despite all that, my work got her killed and almost got you killed, too." His gaze rose to meet mine. "And you mean more to me."

All this time I'd believed I was competing with the memory of a perfect woman.

He shrugged. "The consequences really should have been a series of revenge fucks. But I couldn't get what she'd done out of my head. This nagging doubt that I was never enough for her. This guilt for causing her death."

And only Cameron had the skills to unravel the complexity of grief, betrayal, guilt, as well as his self-hate.

"Cameron never told me," I said.

"What am I to you, Scarlet? Please tell me I'm more than a client."

"I love you." I stepped forward and hugged him.

"Promise me I'm the only man that gets to touch you."

He was right, of course. So many dommes and subs committed to each another, agreeing to play with each other only and not share themselves sexually with other clients. What they'd found fulfilled them on every level and their bond became too precious to jeopardize. Even Cameron had pulled back on the partying when he seriously dated.

I cupped Ethan's face. "I'll hand my clients over to Lotte. I'll remain at Enthrall to oversee the place, make sure it runs well. Is that okay?"

"Thank you."

"Richard can take care of most of the other details and we'll reassess my position."

"Maybe…?"

"Yes?"

"Maybe just have female clients?"

"That wouldn't bother you?"

"Can I be the only one who gets to have sex with you?" He shrugged. "Call me old-fashioned but I'm new to all this…as you know."

"There's still that issue we've not yet discussed."

"Where we're going to live? I'll give up my place. That won't be difficult."

Wow.

"I wasn't even thinking that far ahead."

"That's not what you meant?"

"I'm going to need to be my authentic self."

"I love your authentic self."

"Look, as we're talking long-term, I need to know I'll be fulfilled in this relationship."

He studied me and then lifted the lid to my suitcase. "You know I've never submitted to anyone. Dr. Cole was different. That was for a therapeutic session."

"You know what I am…who I am. I must dominate you, Ethan. If not in life, then at least in the bedroom."

"I don't know how to let you."

"Do you believe we're compatible?"

"If I let you dominate me, will you stay? Spend the rest of the weekend with me? Spend your life with me."

Was he asking me to marry him?

He raised his hands, holding his wrists together.

Desire flooded through me at what he was offering. "I want you to want this, Ethan."

"Cameron told me my therapy took so long because I refused to surrender. I'm assuming surrendering to you will feel different? Obviously."

"Are you mine?"

His swimming trunks revealed an erection.

I picked up his belt buckle that he'd discarded earlier and wrapped it around his wrists, yanking it tight to secure them together.

This was it, a test of compatibility like no other.

We were on the verge of something profound and the call to prove there really could be an *us* was on the line.

He let out a sigh of arousal as I slipped his swimming trunks off his hips. His jaw tightened and his eyelids became heavy. His cock grew harder in the grip of my palm as I caressed him leisurely.

"I'll do anything for you," he whispered.

"Submit entirely." I ran a finger around his tip.

"Oh, Jesus, this is as hot as I remember it from when we were in the dungeon." He was rock hard now and if he expressed any doubt he was enjoying being dominated, his body told me otherwise.

His hands fisted into tight balls as he tried to let go of his power.

"Fully submit and I'm yours," I whispered into his ear.

Our first session had been disrupted by his devilish threats to bring down Chrysalis.

This one would heal us.

We needed this…I needed this. If we were to have any chance of surviving he'd have to learn to become my willing sex slave from time to time and prove he, too, relished in my domme play.

Taking my time I set the scene, making sure the Do Not Disturb sign was on the door, the lighting dimmed and that small gap in the curtains pulled all the way closed. He watched my every move with the laser stare of a hawk, remaining in the center where I'd ordered him to stand and wait patiently, with his wrists bound and his enormous cock arched in desire.

Keeping him revved and ready, I guided him into the shower by holding onto the belt for leverage. We needed to wash this chlorine off. I worked on my own body first, having him in the shower with me but standing back, watching, as I cleansed my body with soap, rubbing the foam over my breasts and between my thighs, lingering teasingly over my sex.

His resistance weakened as he grabbed himself and gave long hard tugs to ease his aching cock.

I gripped his chin, scolding him, and he ceased with a groan of frustration.

Ethan was rewarded for his obedience with my full attention to every part of him, first washing his hair, soaping his body, and then massaging his balls for a while.

"Scarlet." He hissed through clenched teeth.

"Mistress Scarlet."

"Mistress," he said with an edge. "Let me taste you."

"Very well." Reaching up, I scrunched his hair at the scalp and guided him to kneel before me.

I swooned when he buried his face between my thighs, sucking and lapping at my clit and serving me dutifully.

"You've been such a good boy," I purred the words. "Look what you get."

My head rolled back as he continued to devour my sex. Pleasure swirled deep in my core as I tweaked my own nipples.

"Enough," I snapped.

He rested his forehead against my thigh and panted in frustration.

"Up."

He rose majestically.

We stepped out and I took my time drying him with one of the plush towels. I let him dry me, too, and he knew well enough to avoid eye contact and remain subservient. Stretching out the play was a punishment in itself, the sub tortured by restraint, his body thrumming with pleasure.

Removing the belt from his wrists, I coaxed him to lean forward and place his hands on the edge of the sink. Using that same belt, I whipped it across his buttocks until he was rocking forward and backward, moaning, pre-cum hinting at his imminent release, his moans and glazed expression proving he'd slipped into subspace.

"Harder," he demanded. "You know I deserve it."

Exulting in his response, I saw that familiar burning desire in his gaze. His breaths were short and sharp, and proving he could come like this was as much a thrill to me as it was to him, from the way he now and again reached between his legs to jerk-off, balancing with his left hand on the sink to steady his gait.

"Both hands back on the edge," I demanded, pointing.

He complied with a groan of pleasure and I cupped his balls, playing with them.

"You choose my punishment then. Whatever you deem is appropriate."

I tapped his cock. "Better."

He shoved out his ass, offering it to me again, and I knew this call of a newbie sub, this secret desire that all men wanted to ask for but shied away from. After sucking on two fingers to wet them, I gave him what he wanted and slipped them all the way in through that tight puckered ass. His groan was loud and full of yearning.

With my left hand I reached for his cock and set about a rhythmic pace of finger fucking him and jerking him off at the same time. His eyes squeezed shut, jaw slack, hips pumping into my hand and then pushing back to force my fingers deeper.

"Come for me, Mr. Neilson."

He yelled as his cum arched into the air, and I slowed the beat of my fingers to draw out his pleasure, his entire body shuddering, beads of sweat trailing down his spine.

Slipping my fingers out, I caressed his butt cheeks to show my approval.

He looked so adorably dazed, his eyes wide and blinking at me with surprise. "Scarlet, you can dominate me all day long if that's my punishment."

"Stand straight," I snapped.

He straightened his back and placed his hands behind him. "Did I pass the test?" He studied my face, searching to see if he'd pleased me.

As I washed my hands beneath the faucet, I bumped him playfully with my hip. "Wait here."

Returning to the bedroom, I set about uncorking a bottle of chilled Dom Perignon and poured us two crystal flutes of champagne. Carrying them back to the bathroom, I was pleased to find my sub posed just how I'd left him.

I lifted one of the glasses to his lips and let him have a sip. Then I set the glasses down.

Pulling myself up onto the edge of the sink, I spread my legs apart before him. Ethan's gaze was locked on my sex and he looked spellbound, a lick of his lips proving he liked what he saw.

"Mistress?" A plea as his eyes slid down between my thighs.

Dipping my fingertip into one of the glasses, I let a drop of champagne drip over my clit. The sparkling bubbles felt delicious.

With an arched brow I gave Ethan permission to move.

He stepped forward and leaned low, his biceps flexing as he held himself there with his head between my thighs, lapping and sucking and moaning, his tongue searching and finding that delicate liquor. The purposeful sweep of his tongue felt amazing.

Reaching over for the glass, I poured the rest of the champagne over my sex for him and he lapped at it, his eyelids heavy, his panting now furious as he strove to obey—to *please*.

I reached right again and lifted one of the flutes, taking sip after sip of champagne as he continued to lap decadently at my clit, my erotic moans spurring him on. I savored the bubbles, and at the same time, luxuriated in the sensation of having tamed this fierce man.

"Does that taste nice, sub?"

"I'm close to coming again."

"Good boy." I ran my fingers through his dark locks, trembling with luxurious sensations that morphed into an endless climax.

Shuddering out the last of my release, I whispered huskily, "You've made your mistress very happy."

"I need to switch," he said sharply.

"Soon."

"Now." He gave a firm nod. "Please, Scarlet. I need to take control."

Dragging my teeth over my bottom lip, I mulled over his request. "What do you have in mind?"

"Get down from there. It's my turn to fuck you hard. Let me serve you from behind."

A thrill raced up my spine. "Make it count."

He took my glass and set in down, then wrapped his hands around my waist and lifted me off the sink to stand before him.

He spun me around and shoved me forward.

Ethan slapped my butt. "Brace yourself."

"Careful."

"If you suspect I'm giving you another reason to punish me later, you might be right."

"Pleased to hear it."

He slid into me, using my slickness to aid his furious pounding, his hands gripping my hips to garner control.

"Harder," I demanded, shuddering. "I say when you get to come!"

With each thrust he proved we were perfect for each other, two wild souls that fit together, a perfection combination of air and fire.

"Mistress, I'm close."

I let out a long purr.

"Don't make me beg!"

My orgasm stole my breath away, but I sucked in enough air to say, "Come."

Ethan shot his warmth inside me, yelling through his orgasm as he rammed his cock even deeper.

Eventually he grew still, his breaths short and sharp. Mine were ragged as I gasped his name.

He slid out and I turned to face him, already missing our intimate closeness.

Ethan stared into my eyes. "Now do I get to call you mine?"

I gave him a gentle smile. "The first day you entered my dungeon, I knew I would belong to you."

His warm gaze held mine. "So did I."

EPILOGUE

Present Day

"ARE YOU WEARING MY SOCKS AGAIN?" ETHAN STARED AT my feet in mock horror.

He'd shaken me out of my daydream.

I'd been standing in the garden, lost in thought, mulling over how ridiculously happy I felt. We'd been lovers for a year now, and it made me smile that the man who'd tried to destroy me once was now my greatest advocate.

Ethan and I had moved into an elegant Mediterranean-style home in Pacific Palisades six months ago, though only a handful of close friends knew we were together. With his position as a D.A., and my ties to Chrysalis, we'd had to be cautious about who we trusted.

This place was a stone's throw away from Enthrall, and hidden behind a large iron gate to ensure privacy. The panoramic ocean and cove views were breathtaking.

I turned to face Ethan. "I like your socks. They're cozy."

"They look enormous on you." He stepped forward and handed

me a mug of coffee, then took a sip out of his own. "I like you wearing my shirt though."

I loved wearing his shirts at home. They always smelled amazingly like him and made me feel safe.

Ethan wrapped his left arm around my waist.

He really looked stunning in his Armani suit. Tailored to perfection, it showed off his muscular lean frame. He was also wearing my favorite deep gray tie, the one I'd bought him for his birthday. My suave Ethan took my breath away each time he opened his damned mouth.

I sipped my coffee. "Tastes different."

"Decaf."

I let out a long, painful moan.

"You'll survive."

I turned and looked up at him. "How about we invite everyone over? Have a dinner party and announce it."

Ethan placed his hand low on my belly and closed his eyes. "I can feel her moving."

I laughed. "We don't know if she's a she yet. And besides, it's too early to feel any movement."

"We're really having a baby," he said, grinning at me. "She'll take after you and be a little minx."

"Or you and be a complete hardball attorney."

"Maybe it will be twins and we can have one of each."

I thumped his arm playfully, and then said, "Listen, I've been thinking."

"About?"

"Leaving Enthrall. Retiring."

"Do you feel pressured by me?"

"Never. It's the right time."

"Maybe it's time you wrote that romance novel?"

"That's what I was thinking, too. You wouldn't mind a stay-at-home wife?"

"You know what I want. You, happy."

"I'll call Cameron and tell him my plans. He's on New York time, so I'll call him early. I'll tell Richard as soon as I get into Enthrall. He'll be supportive, I just know it."

Ethan gave a nod of approval and turned to walk into the house. "We received something. I opened it. Hope you don't mind."

I followed him back in and he handed me a heavy cream envelope with gold embossed writing.

He gestured to it. "I say we beat them to it."

I raised my gaze to look at him.

"Scarlet, just you and me, saying our vows on the beach. Hawaii, maybe? I can book it today. If you like."

"Are you asking me to marry you?"

"No."

I blinked at him.

"I mean, yes. I mean…I wanted to make sure you liked the idea first before I asked."

"That sounds like a proposal."

"I didn't get the ring yet." He lowered his gaze. "To be totally honest, I saw you standing out there in my socks and I thought, 'I can't live without this woman.'"

I couldn't help grinning.

He stepped forward. "I've been wondering whether I could ever cope with a *no* from you. And worried that, by asking you to be my wife and to commit to us entirely, I might push you away from me. What then? How the fuck could I even exist without you?"

I laughed. "So you're asking for a 'yes' before I say 'yes.'"

"Did I fuck up?"

"Not really."

"I fucked up."

"Go stand in the garden and wait for me."

"Why?" He looked worried.

"Just do it."

We both set our mugs down on the counter and he headed out to the garden, glancing back at me cautiously. It made me smile.

This man made jurors tremble, sent evil criminals away for life, and yet when it came to me he always showed such respect, such love.

Heading into our bedroom, I made my way over to the bedside cabinet and pulled out the small black box. Placing it on top of the envelope, I went back out to the garden.

Ethan's eyes narrowed when he noticed what I was carrying.

I lifted the lid and showed him the fine gold band. "Ethan Neilson, will you marry me?"

"Is that like an engagement ring?"

"Yes."

He beamed as he reached for the band and slipped it onto his left ring finger. "Let's get married this afternoon." He shook his head. "We need a marriage license. I know a judge who can expedite it."

"I like the sound of Hawaii." I set the little black box on the wrought-iron table nearby. "Let's plan a getaway."

"I'm going too fast?"

"You're obsessed with me."

"True." He crushed his lips to mine. "Luckily, you're obsessed with me, too."

"I am."

He hugged me tight. "You said yes."

"Technically, you said yes."

He chuckled. "Will you always boss me around?"

"Would you like that?"

"Yeah."

I felt the proof of his arousal.

"I have to go to work. Don't make me walk into the office like this. I'm already late." He nudged my hand away. "Are you going to open it?"

I arched a brow.

"The envelope, you minx."

I smiled, pulled out the card and read:

You are cordially invited to attend

The Wedding

of

Mia Lauren and Cameron Raif Cole

Ethan watched as I looked over the invitation with happiness. It was going to happen. Mia and Cameron were getting married.

"Let's beat them to it." He wrapped his arms around me.

"Hawaii it is then. Now we just have to decide on an island."

"I've been doing some checking. Lanai sounds amazing. Very private. Just you and me on the beach with the sand between our toes." He kissed the nape of my neck. "There's something else I need to talk to you about."

"Oh?"

"Danton."

My body froze and I stared off at the vast ocean view without really seeing it. The thought of parting with his cello was too terrible to bear. "Ethan, please."

"Here me out."

I forced back my tears. "Okay."

"Let's use Danton as our child's middle name, in memory of him."

I turned and fell into his arms. "You would do that?"

"Scarlet Winters," he said. "When are you going to realize I would do anything for you? I love you more than life itself." He pulled me into a tight embrace. "Danton's the reason I get to have you now."

I felt like I'd waited an entire lifetime for this man, and in many ways I had. Something told me we had Danton's blessing. Those who care about us the most share a piece of their heart with us, giving us what we need to be so much more, their spirit living on through us, their good work enduring an eternity.

"I love you, Ethan, with every part of me. I love you so much."

"So this is what bliss feels like. I've always wondered."

He pressed his lips to mine and I knew I was home.

ALSO BY
VANESSA FEWINGS

THE ENTHRALL SESSIONS
ENTHRALL, ENTHRALL HER, ENTHRALL HIM,
CAMERON'S CONTROL, CAMERON'S CONTRACT,
RICHARD'S REIGN,
ENTHRALL SECRETS, ENTHRALL CLIMAX,
ENTHRALL ECTASY AND ENTHRALL SHADOWS

The ENTHRALL Spin-off series
THE CHANDELIER SESSIONS
CHANDELIER DREAM
CHANDELIER SIN
CHANDELIER ENTHRALLED

THE ICON TRILOGY from Harlequin:
THE CHASE, THE GAME, and THE PRIZE

PANDORA'S PLEASURE
MAXIMUM DARE
PERVADE LONDON and PERVADE MONTEGO BAY
PERFUME GIRL
THE STONE MASTERS VAMPIRE SERIES
THE RAVISHING—With Ava Harrison

ABOUT THE AUTHOR

Vanessa Fewings is the *USA Today* and international bestselling author of the ENTHRALL SESSIONS and THE ICON TRILOGY from HarperCollins along with many additional novels. ENTHRALL has been optioned for film. Her books have been translated into other languages around the world. She now lives on the West Coast with her rescue Foxhound, Sherlock.

vanessafewings.com